Mary swallowed. It was getting dark. The sun had already sunk below the horizon. Twilight was settling over the park. Her eyes remained pinned on Skizz.

"Mary?" Gaia's voice grew urgent. "Do you recognize somebody over by the chess tables?"

"I..."

Skizz lifted his gaze.

He looked directly at Mary. For a terrible instant her body stiffened—petrified in the freezing December air. *I'm dead,* she realized.

As if reading her mind, he smiled and lifted his hand.

Then he drew his forefinger across his throat, very slowly.

Don't miss any books in this thrilling new series
from Pocket Books:

FEARLESS™

All Pocket Book titles are available by post from:
**Simon & Schuster Cash Sales, P.O. Box 29,
Douglas, Isle of Man IM99 1BQ**
Credit cards accepted. Please telephone 01624 836000,
Fax 01624 670923, Internet http://www.bookpost.co.uk
or email: bookshop@enterprise.net for details

FEARLESS™

FRANCINE PASCAL

REBEL

POCKET
BOOKS

An imprint of Simon & Schuster UK Ltd
A Viacom Company
Africa House, 64-78 Kingsway, London WC2B 6AH

Produced by 17th Street Productions, Inc.
33 West 17th Street, New York, NY 10011

A CIP catalogue record for this book is
available from the British Library

ISBN 0671 77341 0

1 3 5 7 9 10 8 6 4 2

Printed by Omnia Books Ltd, Glasgow

Honesty is a funny thing.

People always tell you that they want you to be honest with them. But they're lying. Nobody wants that. Honesty sucks. That's why the word *honesty* is always preceded by other words, like *brutal* and *painful*.

I keep all of my secrets for just that reason. They'd hurt too much if anybody knew. And I don't mean they would just hurt the people I told. I mean they would hurt me, too.

So I keep them to myself. And it's not all that hard. After all, dishonesty kind of runs in my family.

Just look at my father. He ditched me without ever telling me where he was going or why—and he did it on the worst night of my life. And my uncle has apparently been watching over me my entire life, but he never even bothered to introduce himself. He only shows up when I'm about to get shot in the head or stabbed

by some crazed serial killer.
Great, thanks. But I can take
care of myself.

Come to think of it, everybody
I know seems to hide the truth
somehow. Sam. Ella. Even Mary. In
fact, the only person I can think
of who *doesn't* hide the truth is
Ed Fargo. He's honest about
everything.

But as far as keeping secrets
goes, I have to admit, I really
take first prize. I've never told
Sam how I feel about him. And
that's just scratching the surface. I've never told him or anyone else about my total inability
to feel fear. Or why I'm trained
to kick almost anyone's ass in
about three seconds flat. Or why
I'm stuck with George and Ella.

And here's the biggest one of
all. I've never told anyone about
my dad or about my mother's
death. But I have a good reason.
If I were totally honest with my
friends about my past . . . well,
I'd put their lives in danger. I

already have. More than once.

Maybe everyone has a reason
for hiding the truth. After all,
honesty seems to create more
problems than it solves. It can
hurt. It can even kill. I guess
that's why people are afraid of
the truth.

But I wouldn't know about
that. I'm not afraid of anything.

His body
went limp.
He wouldn't
try to
move. She
knew
it. He'd
tasted
an
excruciating
pain. . . .

**her
kind
of
game**

SKELETONS.

The Three Wise Men

That's exactly what the trees in Washington Square Park looked like at this time of night: spindly, grotesque skeletons. At least that was how they looked to Gaia Moore. It was amazing how a place could feel like an amusement park one month and a cemetery the next. But that was New York City. It was constantly changing, and often not for the better. That could be said of a lot of things, actually—Gaia's life included.

"Why does this park totally die right before Christmas?" Mary suddenly asked of nobody in particular.

Gaia smirked. One of the coolest things about Mary Moss was that she had an uncanny knack for saying exactly what Gaia was thinking. She also shared the same intolerance for bullshit.

"Because there's no action down here," Ed said. His breath made little white clouds in the frigid December air. "The real action is in Midtown. I say we buy some little red suits and pom-pom hats, then go volunteer to be elves outside some big megastore, like Macy's."

"I'm too tall to be an elf," Gaia replied.

"Me too," Mary added.

Ed shrugged. Dead leaves crunched under his

wheelchair. "Then we'll get some fake beards for you guys. Instead of being elves we'll be the three wise men."

Gaia had to laugh. The three wise men. That was funny. A wheelchair-bound ex–skate rat, a female ex–coke addict, and . . . *her*. Whatever Gaia was. She probably *could* pass for a man. Easily. She wasn't beautiful and skinny like Mary. Nope. Forget a wise man; Gaia had the body of a prizefighter. She didn't even need the beard. All she needed was a little five o'clock shadow. Now that she thought about it, the only remotely feminine aspect of her appearance was her unkempt mane of blond hair. But there was probably a direct correlation between one's freakish looks and the swirling mess inside one's head, wasn't there?

"I guess it's too cold for any Christmas pageantry, anyway," Ed mumbled.

Ed was right. It was too cold for anything. Even chess. Gaia had never seen the park this quiet or deserted. Usually *some* die-hard chess fanatic was out at the tables, trying to hustle a game, no matter what the weather. Like Mr. Haq. Or her old friend Zolov. But Gaia hadn't seen a whole lot of Zolov since he'd been slashed by those neo-Nazi idiots who used to hang around the miniature Arc de Triomphe on the north side.

She almost *wished* a few skinheads were around

just so the place would feel more like home. In fact, she wouldn't mind at all if one of them jumped out of the shadows and tried to attack her. She'd walked this park many times for that exact reason. But seeking combat wasn't a group activity. It was something she did on her own. In secrecy. Besides, at this moment she wasn't really craving a good fight. No, what she really missed right now were the sounds and smells of months past: the gurgling of the fountain, the laughter of the NYU students, the sweet odor of roasted peanuts. . . .

Mary abruptly stopped in her tracks.

"You know what? We *should* do something to liven things up." She adjusted her black wool cap and brushed a few wayward red curls out of her eyes. "It's winter break. We're free. I say we create a little excitement of our own."

Gaia met Mary's gaze. She knew that gleam in Mary's green eyes all too well. It whispered: *Let's do something crazy.* And in a way, Gaia could empathize. After all, courting danger was one of her favorite pastimes, too. But Mary's reckless tendencies led down a much more self-destructive path than Gaia's own.

Then again, some people might argue that deliberately looking for fights was a hell of a lot worse than snorting a big fat line of white powder up your nose. But Gaia had never paid any attention to other people's opinions. Ever.

"Why don't I like the sound of that at all?" Ed muttered.

Mary laughed. "Come on, you guys. We're here in New York City. By the looks of things, we basically have the place to ourselves." She waved her hands at the empty benches and frozen pavement. "I mean, everyone else is holed up in their apartments or vacationing in the Hamptons or doing whatever it is that normal people do."

"Your point being?" Ed asked.

"That I'm bored!" Mary cried. "I don't do drugs anymore, so I have to find *something* to do, right?" She laughed.

Gaia kept quiet. Unfortunately, the joke wasn't very funny. Mary had only been off cocaine since Thanksgiving, and Gaia knew enough about drugs to know that a lot of addicts relapsed in those first precarious weeks of clean living. Especially when they were bored.

"I don't know," Ed said quietly. He fidgeted in his wheelchair, tapping his gloved fingers on the armrests. "If you ask me, a little boredom is a good thing. Anyway, aren't we supposed to be going to Gaia's house right now?"

Ed was right. They *were* on their way to the Nivens' house (Gaia never thought of it as her own, and she never would), but there was really nothing to do there. Gaia shook her head. Poor Ed. Part of her agreed with him. Ever since he'd met Gaia, Ed's life had been a little too exciting. Kidnappings. Serial killers. Random acts of violence. Part of her wanted to protect him—to shield him from the danger that surrounded her at all times.

But the other part of her—she couldn't ignore—was just as bored as Mary. Besides, if Mary was looking for a way to keep her mind off drugs, Gaia was all for it. After all, Mary had appointed her to help out with getting involved in "good, clean fun." Whatever that was.

"What do you have in mind?" Gaia asked Mary.

Mary raised her eyebrows. "A little game," she said. She smiled down at Ed, then back at Gaia. "What do you guys think about truth or dare?"

Ed snickered. "Ooh. That sounds *really* exciting. Can we play spin the bottle next?"

Mary ignored him. "Gaia?" she prompted. "What do you say?"

"Sure," Gaia said. It actually *did* sound exciting—at least to her. The fact of the matter was that she had never played truth or dare before. *Or* spin the bottle. Or any other games that normal kids would have played, the ones who didn't have twisted secret agents for fathers.

But that was the great thing about hanging out with Mary. She introduced Gaia to all kinds of normal experiences. And always in a very abnormal way.

ED FARGO'S BIGGEST PROBLEM WASN'T what most people might think: namely, that his legs would never work again. No. He'd learned to deal with that. Or at least *accept* it. It was just another part of his life now. An unpleasant part, sure—like suffering through history class, or seeing his ex-girlfriend Heather Gannis every single day, or forcing himself to smile back at all the phony bastards who pretended to take pity on him. But it wasn't *torture.* No, Ed Fargo's biggest problem was that he couldn't say no to Gaia Moore.

That was torture.

Even more tortuous (or pathetic) was that he was completely, utterly, one hundred percent in love with her. And she had absolutely no clue.

On more than one occasion he'd almost mustered the courage to tell her. He'd even gone so far as to compose a few e-mails and letters, but he always tore them up or deleted them at the last minute. A voice inside inevitably reminded him that it was better to live with delusional hope than crushing rejection.

God. One of these days he was really going to have to shut that voice up.

But for now, it looked like he was resigned to following Gaia around like a dog and catering to her every whim. Unfortunately, this frequently involved getting into fights, or ducking bullets, or discovering secrets that were probably best left buried.

As every lame-ass soap opera was quick to point out, love sucked.

"So what do you say we get started?" Mary asked.

"Can we at least play at Gaia's house?" Ed groaned. His teeth started chattering. It wasn't from cold, either. The park didn't exactly fill him with a sense of safety and well-being. He'd almost been *murdered* here. He peered into the shadowy tangle of barren tree limbs that lined the path on either side. "We're all freezing our butts off, in case you forgot."

Mary shook her head. "I say we start here. Gaia?"

"No better time than the present," Gaia agreed.

It figured neither of them would listen to him. And he wasn't about to leave without them, either. He really *was* a dog. Woof, woof.

"So who goes first?" he grumbled.

"We'll shoot for it," Mary said. "Rock, scissors, paper." She stuck her hand behind her back. "On three . . ."

Great, Ed thought. He hated rock, scissors, paper almost as much as truth or dare. With his luck, he'd probably lose—and they would dare him to strip naked and streak up Fifth Avenue in his wheelchair.

Mary smiled. "One . . . two . . . three . . ."

Ed extended a fist: rock. It always seemed safest, although somebody smarter—like Gaia—might disagree.

His eyes flashed to Gaia's hand. *Ha!* Scissors. He glanced at Mary. Rock, too. Unbelievable.

Gaia Moore had actually lost.

It was probably the first time he'd seen Gaia lose at anything. He couldn't help but smile. Maybe this wouldn't be so bad after all. It would be nice to see her do something ridiculous, wouldn't it?

"Oh, Jesus." Gaia moaned.

"Now, don't be a sore loser," Mary teased, winking at Ed.

"So which is it?" Ed asked gleefully. "Truth or dare?"

Gaia pursed her lips. "Dare. And you don't have to ask me again. It's dare for the duration of the game."

Mary clapped. "Perfect."

She turned back toward the arch. A solitary figure was sitting on one of the benches, wrapped in a scarf with a hat pulled low over his eyes—a skinny and grizzled older man Ed had never seen before. Ed's excitement began to fade. He could see where this was going. He should have known Gaia would never pick truth. He also should have known Mary would dare Gaia to take some inane, meaningless risk. Why did the two of them have to *create* trouble? Why did they have to pluck it out of thin air? He held his breath as Mary raised her hand and pointed at the figure.

"I dare you to go kiss that guy," she said.

The Good Thing about Rats

TRUTH OR DARE WAS RIGHT UP GAIA'S alley. She could tell right away that she would be able to add it to that short list of loves that made her life tolerable. Everything else on the list was food related. Well, she loved a good chess match. And Sam. But there was no point in dwelling on *that*.

What she really loved were diversions.

She loved anything that distracted her from the dismal specifics of her existence. And kissing some random stranger in the park certainly qualified as a diversion, didn't it?

She walked toward him on the darkened path, waiting for him to look up and notice her. But he didn't move. He was slumped on the bench. His legs were spread in front of him, his skeletal chest rising and falling in the even rhythm of sleep. Icy puffs of breath drifted away from his open mouth. Gaia's nose wrinkled. *Yuck.* Maybe he was drunk. Or *something.* She'd be sure to ask him if she could just kiss him on the forehead—

Wait a second.

He wasn't asleep. He was just pretending.

Only someone with Gaia's acute awareness in sizing up a potential opponent could detect the subtle clues of consciousness: the exaggerated way he exhaled, the concentrated stillness of his eyelids. So he was lying in wait. Setting a trap. The asshole was waiting to attack her.

A familiar electric energy shot through Gaia's body—the jolt that always came in place of fear. This was going to be even more fun than she had expected. How come she'd never thought of playing this game before? It was tailor-made for somebody with Gaia's unique condition: somebody who felt only a sublime emptiness in the face of any threat.

Let's see what you can do, she silently taunted as she stepped in front of him.

She placed her feet squarely between his own. A smile played on her lips. Yes, she could see the tension building in his arms as they lay at his sides. His breathing quickened—just a little. He was getting ready to make his move. To take her by surprise.

Gaia glanced back at Mary and Ed. They were a good thirty yards away, silhouetted against the leafless trees. Their expressions were unreadable in the darkness. She gave them a quick thumbs-up. Then she caught a whiff of bourbon and winced. Disgusting. But she had to get it over with. Otherwise she would lose—and losing was something she was not prepared to do. Fearlessness had to serve *some* purpose, even if it was for a game. And besides, this jerk needed to be taught a lesson. Gaia *lived* for teaching bullies lessons. She was committed.

"Excuse me, sir?" Gaia bent over to look into his eyes.

Two hands clasped around her wrists.

"Gotcha!" the man cried.

She almost laughed. "Give me a break," she mumbled disappointedly. It figured he would grab her by the arms. It was the most obvious and idiotic form of attack. But she'd let him enjoy the illusion of control for a second or two. His thick fingers dug through the fibers of her coat.

"Now what do you think you're doing?" he asked.

She didn't answer. Instead she just gazed into his haggard face. Talk about disgusting. His skin looked like an oil field. He must have been fifty years old. His beady black eyes were rheumy with alcohol.

"You wanna play with me?" he hissed, laughing. He gave her arms a sudden yank, pulling her closer. "Well, it's your lucky night, sugar. I'm gonna warm you up. I'm gonna give you something you'll never forget."

Gaia rolled her eyes. She only had to remember creeps like Charlie Salita and his rapist friend,

15

Sideburns Tim, to feel a surge of anger. But this guy was just too pathetic for any kind of major confrontation. And even though she wanted to prolong this encounter—just for the sake of excitement—the stink of this guy's breath and body were enough to make her puke. Too bad. Sighing, she stamped the heel of her combat boot on the man's toes.

"What the—"

A shocked whimper escaped his lips. His hold on her instantly loosened. Quick as a flash, she clasped his right hand against her left forearm. His eyes bulged. With a single deft maneuver she flipped him off the bench to the ground at her feet—flat on his back.

"What the hell?" he gasped.

He tried to wriggle free, but Gaia held his hand fast. She bent it back slightly.

"Ow!" he screamed.

His body went limp. He wouldn't try to move. She knew it. He'd tasted an excruciating pain. That was the beauty of this particular grip. She could snap his wrist in a second, but there was no need to injure him. It was the essence of true kung fu and one of the first lessons her father had taught her: the art of intimidation—the art of threatening torture without actually having to inflict it more than once.

"Now, you aren't going to try this with anyone else, are you?" Gaia asked calmly.

16

He didn't answer. He gazed up at her, wild-eyed. His breath came quickly. Even though the temperature was below freezing, she could see beads of sweat forming on his bulbous nose.

"Are you?" she persisted.

"No!" he grunted, cringing. "Come on! Lemme go! Lemme go, you bitch!"

Gaia frowned. "What did you call me?"

"Nothing." His eyes squeezed shut. "Just lemme go," he pleaded. "I'm sorry. . . ."

"That's better," she said. "Now I'll let you go. Just as soon as you promise me you won't try to grab some other girl who—"

"Gaia!" Ed's voice sliced through the night air.

Oh, brother. Once again her self-appointed Superman was swooping in to save the day. Why did Ed always try to get involved? He was undeniably brave and undeniably sweet, but he must have had a short-term memory problem. He'd seen her kick a dozen scumbags' asses, and *this* situation was certainly under control—yet he was still racing down the path as fast as the chair would carry him, with Mary close on his heels. They made quite a rescue party. She almost smiled.

"Come on," the guy at her feet murmured one last time.

Gaia glanced back down at him. "Fine," she said in a soft voice. "But if I ever see you in this park again, I'll think twice about letting you get off so easy." Her tone was very matter-of-fact, as if she were explaining the rules of chess. "Got it?"

He nodded. His face was etched with what Gaia knew, intellectually, was fear. She let go of his hands, then leaned over and lifted him by the lapels of his coat. Jesus. He even was heavier than he looked. She shoved him out on the path and watched as he scurried away.

A rat, she realized. That's exactly what he looked like. A big, fat rat.

But one who'd learned never to proposition another teenage girl again.

Yes. The good thing about rats was that they could be easily trained. All they needed was a little nega-tive reinforcement.

"Gaia?" Ed gasped breathlessly, skidding to a halt. "Are you all right?"

She turned around. "I think I'll live," she said, trying not to smile.

"Holy shit!" Mary cried delightedly. She doubled over beside Ed. Her lungs were heaving. "That was *awesome*. What did he try to do to you, anyway?"

Gaia shrugged. "He told me he'd give me something I'd never forget," she replied. But as she spoke the words, a wave of exhaustion swept over her.

Without thinking, she slumped down on the park bench.

Her face twisted in a scowl. It was ridiculous: Even after a fight as pathetic as *that* one, she still felt completely drained. She supposed she should learn to expect it. Her body was like a balloon. In combat it would fill up with adrenaline and strength—and then *pop!*—it would deflate. Instantly. For a few minutes she would be unable to move. And somehow this peculiar handicap always managed to slip her mind when she was fighting someone. Maybe because she'd never understood it.

"Are you *sure* you're all right?" Ed asked, peering at her closely.

"Fine," she whispered. She shook her head.

After a few seconds her strength began to return. It flowed slowly into her arms and legs, filling them like a thick potion.

She dusted off her hands and stood.

She found herself smiling again.

In spite of the stench, kissing that guy had been a lot of fun. In a very weird way. It had been very diverting, too. She hadn't thought about Sam or her father or any other stupid crap at all during those precious few moments. Truth or dare was *definitely* her kind of game. It helped her to forget. And forgetting was a very, very good thing.

"So," she said, glancing at Ed and Mary. "Whose turn is it now?"

UNDER NORMAL CIRCUMSTANCES, ED WOULD
have loved hanging out with
two beautiful girls.

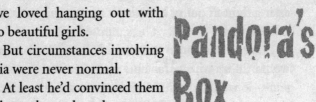

But circumstances involving
Gaia were never normal.

At least he'd convinced them
to leave the park and retreat to
the cozy warmth of Gaia's brownstone. That was *something*.

Now, however, he would probably drive himself
crazy staring at Gaia and Mary as they lounged side by
side on the overstuffed living-room couch. Any beautiful girl had a habit of driving Ed crazy these days—and
not just Gaia. Yup. The needle was continuously pop-
ping into red on the Fargo lust-o-meter. But he was
good at hiding his lecherous thoughts. It
was a skill he'd cultivated carefully since the accident.
That was something, too.

"All right, Ed, it's your turn," Gaia announced.

He shook his head. "You actually want to keep
playing?"

"Why wouldn't I?"

"Gee, I don't know," he said, with as much sarcasm
as he could manage. "Maybe because somebody just
attacked you."

"Oh, please." She waved her hand dismissively.
"That was nothing."

He wanted to argue, but there probably wasn't

much point. For Gaia, flipping that guy on his ass and scaring the hell out of him *was* nothing. He'd seen her do a lot worse.

"I say we go back out there," Mary said. She sat up straight, peeking distractedly through the windows out to Perry Street. "Being cooped up inside is so lame. It's not *that* cold. As long as we keep moving around, we'll be fine."

Ed slouched back in his wheelchair. "Um . . . haven't you guys forgotten about the truth part of this game? If everyone picks truth, we'll be fine. We won't have to do anything stupid."

"Forget it," Gaia stated. She shook her head vehemently. "You can't tell people what to pick. That ruins the point of the game." She smiled at him. "And for making such a lame suggestion, I say that you have to go next."

Mary turned away from the window. "I second that motion," she said, grinning wickedly.

Ed sighed. So much for trying to be clever. He should know better by now.

"Fine." He groaned. "Then I pick truth."

But as soon as he closed his mouth, he began to regret his decision. This was probably going to suck. Big time. Gaia wasn't going to sugarcoat a "truth" for him. No. She never sugarcoated anything. She wasn't the least bit concerned about sparing his feelings.

21

Of course, that was what he loved most about her.

Other people acted extra kind because he was in a wheelchair. Or they just pretended to ignore the chair altogether. But Gaia did neither. She was too honest to be polite. So was Mary. It was no wonder they got along so well.

"Truth, eh?" Gaia asked. She exchanged a quick glance with Mary. There was a sparkle in her eye. "All right, Ed Fargo." She looked him straight in the face. "Did you and Heather ever do the nasty?"

His jaw tightened.

Dammit.

He was starting to remember why he hated this game so much. It figured Gaia would mention Heather. Right. It figured because he never would have expected it. Why *would* she bring up Heather? Gaia hated Heather. And vice versa. They had a perfectly reciprocal relationship. Yin and yang.

And there was also the unpleasant fact that Heather was currently dating Sam, the guy whom Gaia loved.

But that was Gaia for you. She was a Pandora's box of surprises. Always walking that fine line between psychopath and friend. She never seemed completely satisfied unless the air was thick with tension—or if she was in danger of getting herself hurt.

"Well?" Gaia prodded.

Ed chewed his lip. There was another reason this question sucked so much.

He'd never told anyone about his sex life.

He and Heather *had* lost their virginity to each other, only weeks before the accident . . . but they had made a pact to keep it secret. It was their business. Theirs alone. And in spite of the fact that they had broken up over two years ago, Ed still treasured the memory enough to honor that pact. He wouldn't violate it for the sake of a stupid game, even if it pissed off Gaia.

"I changed my mind," Ed finally said. "I want to pick dare."

"No way," Mary interjected. She shook her head. "That's against the rules."

Gaia blinked. For an instant Ed caught her gaze.

Her face softened. "No, that's all right. We'll let the rules slide this time." She grinned. "But just this once."

Ed sighed, relaxing a little bit. That was Gaia for you, too. Just when you thought you'd lost her to the dark side forever, she pulled off some little miracle to let you know there was a heart in there somewhere—buried deep under that impenetrable shell.

"You know what? I actually think I've gotta split," he lied. "It's late. My parents start worrying. You know?"

"Sure," Gaia said softly.

"I don't know," Mary teased. "Sounds like a cop-out to me."

Whatever, Ed thought. Let Mary think it was a

cop-out. At this point he didn't really care. Gaia understood. That was all that mattered.

He turned his chair toward the door. Luckily Gaia's brownstone was one of the tiny minority of houses in Manhattan that were actually wheelchair friendly. Making a quick getaway would be easy.

"Hey, wait a second," Mary said. "What do you say we pick up where we left off tomorrow? That way we can play outside again—when it's light out and warmer." Her voice became excited. "We can use all of New York City as a playing field."

Ed glanced over his shoulder. "I don't know," he said doubtfully. "I mean—"

"Come on, Ed," Gaia interrupted. "What else are you gonna do?"

That was a good question. He knew the answer, too. He was going to sit alone in his house all day long and think about her. And that was just too sad to think about. Not to mention pathetic.

"So are you in or are you out?" Mary demanded impatiently.

Ed sighed. "I'm in," he mumbled.

At the very least, he'd be able to keep an eye on her. Maybe he'd even be able to keep her from doing something incredibly risky or stupid.

Maybe he'd even save her life.

Yeah, right. He could try, anyway. The way he always did. That was also something. Wasn't it?

To: L
From: ELJ
Date: December 22
File: 776244
Subject: Gaia Moore
Last Seen: Perry Street residence, 11:23 P.M.

Update: Subject observed again with new compan-
ion, Mary Moss. Seems to be developing an emotional attachment. Preliminary intelligence
indicates Moss is a recovering substance abuser.
My own observations lead me to believe she nur-
tures subject's disregard for authority or personal safety. Advise.

To: ELJ
From: L
Date: December 23
File: 776422
Subject: Gaia Moore

Directives: Continue to monitor Moss's interac-
tion with subject. I will monitor as well.
Neutralization may be required if she places subject in danger. Await further instructions.

I used to think that having a best friend or soul mate or whatever you want to call it was a load of fairy-tale crap. Best friends exist only on TV shows. As far as I was concerned, nobody could get close to another person in real life. People are just too phony. Or evil. Or self-interested. If somebody becomes your friend, it's usually because they want something in return.

As I said, that's what I used to think. But that was back when I was doing about three grams of coke a day.

It's funny, because I had a lot of friends back then. Tons. They just weren't real. Some of them knew about my habit, and some didn't. It didn't matter, though. I was high all the time. I put on an act with everybody. I used to feel like I had a magic bag full of invisible masks—and I just would change into a different one, depending on the situation. My real face never showed. To be honest, I didn't even know what my real face was or if I even had one.

But then I met Gaia Moore. Or to be more specific, she exploded into my life.

For starters, she beat the crap out of Skizz, the asshole coke dealer who was about to pump a bullet into my stomach. I've never seen anything like it. She was like some kind of fighting machine. There I was, trapped in the park—facing down the barrel of a gun—and all of a sudden this mass of blond hair appears out of nowhere, belts Skizz a few times, and then sends him running away. Then she collapsed. Quite an introduction, huh? At least she let me buy her a cup of coffee.

But after that, I felt like there was a magnet pulling me toward her. I couldn't stop thinking about her. I was fascinated—and a little confused, too, because she didn't seem to want anything from

me. She never has. Except for me
to quit doing drugs.

It's strange. Those first few
days after I stopped using cocaine, I used to think that there
was no way I'd be able to func-
tion without it. I was convinced
I would have to hide myself away
from the rest of the world for
the rest of my life.

But when I'm with Gaia, something happens to me. It's almost
as if all my fear just melts away
and evaporates into thin air.
Seriously. I'm fearless. I can do
anything. And the rush I get from
hanging out with her is a hell of
a lot more real and intense than
the buzz I got from doing a couple of lines.

Not to say that life is
peachy. My problems aren't over.
For one thing, my family doesn't
trust me. Why should they? I lied
to them for years. They thought I
was the perfect daughter. Little
did they know. So now they watch
me the way a guard would watch a

dangerous prisoner. A nice group
of guards, but still.

And even though I left the
world of cocaine behind, other
people haven't. I still owe Skizz
five hundred bucks. People like
Skizz don't forgive debts. It's
bad for their business.

I guess that's another reason
I like hanging around with Gaia
so much. She makes me feel safe.

For a terrible instant her body stiffened—petrified in **the coolest** freezing December air. *I'm dead*, she realized.

"TRUTH OR DARE?" MARY ASKED.

The Face in the Crowd

Gaia rolled her eyes. "I *told* you, Mary. You don't need to ask me. I'm not gonna pick truth. Ever. Under any circumstances." She smiled. "Got it?"

Mary shook her head. She glanced down at Ed. She could tell that he was getting frustrated, too. This was ridiculous. They had been wandering around downtown for almost three hours, and Gaia still hadn't picked truth. What would it take, anyway? A gun to her head? Well . . . no, that probably wouldn't work, either.

The problem was, the girl had a pathological aversion to revealing any information about herself. The only reason Mary had suggested this game in the first place was to answer all the tantalizing Gaia questions that had festered in her mind over the past seven weeks. Like why Gaia's parents were out of the picture. Or where she had lived before New York. Or how she had learned to fight like Wonder Woman meets Jackie Chan. Or what the *real* deal was between Gaia and Heather Gannis's boyfriend, Sam Moon . . .

Or why she seemed so certain that she could die at any moment.

"So?" Gaia prompted, clearly enjoying herself. "What's it gonna be?"

Mary glanced at Ed again, who shrugged. They were having fun, but this was starting to bug the hell out of her. There was only one solution. She had to dare Gaia to do something so over the top that there would be no *way* she could pull it off. But that posed another problem. So far, Gaia had eaten a dozen doughnuts in less than a minute (without barfing) and done a handstand on the median of the West Side Highway (without dying). And smiled the whole time.

She had to have a breaking point, though. Everyone did.

Mary shoved her hands into her pockets and glanced into the northwest entrance of Washington Square Park. Somehow they always managed to end up here. She didn't have the slightest clue why, either. The place wasn't exactly hopping with action. It was gray and cold and miserable. The sun was beginning to fade. A few heavily bundled old men were huddled around the chess tables, but that was it.

She supposed she could always dare Gaia to kiss one of them and watch another fight. Nah. Been there, done that . . .

"I got it," Ed said. He turned his wheelchair back toward Waverly Place and pointed at a little Italian restaurant on the opposite corner, La Cocina. It wasn't more than a hundred feet away. There was a table full of thirty-something yuppies in the window: bloated Wall Street types who had probably left work early to get a head start on the night's drinking. The West Village was filled with people like that at this time of year—people who had a convenient excuse to get drunk earlier and more often than usual because it was "the holiday season." Mary knew all about that excuse, which was another reason she wanted to get out of here. The holiday spirit could get ugly fast. Guys like that inevitably got rowdy and leered at her. Or worse.

Ed glanced back at Gaia. He smiled. "I dare you to streak those guys."

Mary laughed. She hadn't been expecting *that*.

"But it's, like, twenty-eight degrees outside right now," Gaia said, frowning.

"Chicken, huh?" Ed lifted his shoulders. His smile widened. "Then I guess you lose."

Gaia started laughing, too. "You really want me to take off all my clothes and run past that window?"

"I wouldn't ask you if I didn't," he replied casually.

"But . . ." Gaia glanced at Mary.

"But what?" Mary folded her arms across her chest and raised her eyebrows. No way was she going to cut Gaia any slack. Ed was a smart guy. If Gaia refused to do this, then she would have to pick truth.

"What if I get arrested?" Gaia protested.

Mary waved her hands around the street. "I don't see any cops." She looked at Ed. "Do you?"

Ed shook his head. "Nope."

"Fine," Gaia grumbled. She quickly ducked into the park and disappeared behind some bushes.

"I don't believe this," Ed muttered.

Mary shook her head. "Neither do I, really."

She stared at the mass of prickly leaves—the only trace of green left in the park—wondering if Gaia was really stripping off all her clothes back there. It *was* freezing. Mary rubbed her arms against her sides. Maybe this wasn't such a hot idea. If Gaia really did go through with this, there was a very good chance that she'd catch pneumonia.

Mary's eyes narrowed. She took a step forward. Gaia was definitely doing *something*—

"Holy shit!" Ed yelled.

Before the image could even fully register in Mary's mind, she saw Gaia in midair: jumping over the fence onto the sidewalk—wearing nothing but her hat. Mary's jaw fell open. She heard Ed gasp as she stood gaping at the pale, muscular frame and the wild mane of blond hair trailing behind it.

Without pausing to look for any oncoming traffic, Gaia sprinted across the street to the window, knocked on it, and jumped up and down a few times.

Every single guy at that table looked like he had just been slapped.

"Awesome!" Ed yelled. He clapped and clasped his stomach, laughing hysterically.

In spite of her shock and mild horror, Mary found she was smiling, too. So were the guys at the table. Then *they* started clapping. It figured. But Gaia had already beat a hasty retreat back behind the bushes. The whole trip had taken no more than ten seconds.

Damn, that girl was impressive. There was nothing Gaia Moore wouldn't do. Absolutely nothing.

Mary sighed. She glanced around to make sure there were no cops in sight. It was probably a good idea to get out of here. Maybe they should head uptown. Yeah. To Mary's neighborhood. The Upper East Side. The land of the rich and famous. There was plenty of havoc to wreak up there—

Oh my God.

Mary's heart jumped. In an instant she forgot all about Gaia.

Skizz.

He was here. In the park. Among the chess gawkers. The long, grayish brown beard was unmistakable. His head was down and his gaze fixed to one of the tables . . . but she could still see that tangled mop of hair, those beady brown eyes.

"Mary?" Ed asked. The voice seemed to float to her from another universe. "Are you all right?"

"I . . . I . . ." She shook her head. Her feet were stuck to the pavement. She couldn't move. Did Skizz know she was here? Had he been spying on her? He could have been following her this whole time, waiting to make a move—

Something brushed her back. She flinched.

"Whoa," Ed murmured. He raised his hands. "Sorry. I just wanted to see what you were looking at." He moved closer to Mary in an effort to follow her line of sight. "What is it?"

Finally she willed herself to take a few steps back. "We—uh, we gotta get out of here," she stammered. "It's not . . . it's not . . ."

"It's not *what?*" he whispered.

"Safe," she croaked.

Ed cleared his throat. "Um, Mary? You're starting to freak me out a little. Did a cop see Gaia?"

Mary couldn't answer. She could only stare at the beard and `that fat, foul stomach.`

A moment later Gaia ducked back out from behind the bushes—flushed and slightly disheveled. Her coat was unbuttoned, and her shoes were unlaced. She raised her hand in triumph, then paused.

"What's going on?" she asked.

"We gotta split," Mary found herself answering.

"What do you mean?" Gaia asked, glancing back toward the park.

Mary swallowed. It was getting dark. The sun had already sunk below the horizon. Twilight was settling over the park. Her eyes remained pinned on Skizz.

"Mary?" Gaia's voice grew urgent. "Do you recognize somebody over by the chess tables?"

"I . . ."

Skizz lifted his gaze.

He looked directly at Mary. For a terrible instant her body stiffened—petrified in the freezing December air. *I'm dead,* she realized.

As if reading her mind, he smiled and lifted his hand.

Then he drew his forefinger across his throat, very slowly.

"No," she whispered. She squeezed her eyes shut, half convinced that this was some terrible hallucination, some all too vivid nightmare.

Mary forced herself to open her eyes again. She blinked a few times. *What the—*

He was gone. Just like that. Vanished. Somehow that was even more terrifying than if he had hung around. Her gaze darted from face to face among the group at the chess tables, then up and down the various paths. She caught a glimpse of a hunched figure who might have been him, scurrying up toward Fifth Avenue . . . but she couldn't be sure. *Jesus.* Pent-up air flowed from her lungs. Her shoulders sagged.

"Can you please tell us what's going on?" Ed demanded.

Mary leaned on the back of his wheelchair for support. Her knees were wobbly. "It's nothing," she whispered. "I'm sorry. He . . . uh, he's not there anymore." She couldn't keep from shivering.

"Who?" Ed asked impatiently.

Mary glanced at Gaia. Had she seen?

There was no reason to dig up the past. They were having so much fun. There was no reason for Ed and Gaia to know that she was `paranoid about drug-crazed stalkers from coke deals gone bad.`

Gaia chewed her lip for a moment. Her blond hair flapped in the bitter wind.

"Are you sure you're okay?" she said finally. She flashed Mary a quick smile. "Do you want to get out of here?"

And at that moment Mary realized something that she never had before: Having a friend meant being able to communicate without having to speak a word.

"RIDING THE SUBWAY AT NIGHT IS DANGEROUS."

It was one of those myths about New York City that Gaia had never understood. Like the one about how all New Yorkers talked with a ridiculous accent, `like mobsters.` Almost all of those myths were lies. She could hardly think of a safer place than the Uptown East Side number 6 local train. For one

Miraculous Zit-related Promises

thing, there was plenty of light. The glare of those harsh fluorescent lights was practically blinding. And the subways were always *somewhat* crowded, no matter what the hour. They were also crawling with cops.

On the other hand, some lunatic could shove you onto the tracks or a pickpocket could snatch your wallet. And the cops were mostly slobs—stuffed to the gills with doughnuts and coffee. A lot could go wrong if a person was unprepared. Maybe it wasn't so much that the subways were dangerous. Maybe it was just that they were a playground of the unexpected.

That was why Gaia loved them so much.

"Do you think Ed's pissed at me?" Mary asked over the rhythmic roar of the train wheels.

Gaia shook her head, leaning back in the plastic seat. The only drag about the subway was that it was impossible to get comfortable. She inevitably found herself getting mushed next to somebody with terminal BO. And her butt always went to sleep. But at least the car was relatively empty.

"Why would he be pissed?" Gaia asked.

"Because I want to go uptown. And, you know . . ." She didn't finish.

Yes, Gaia knew. Mary felt guilty because going uptown meant ditching Ed. It was nearly impossible for guy in a wheelchair to ride the train.

"Believe me, Ed is psyched we left him behind,"

Gaia said. "He was looking for an excuse to go home. I think he's had about enough of truth or dare. He probably would have been bummed if we'd taken a bus or a cab because that would have meant he had to come with us."

"Maybe." But Mary didn't look so sure. She sighed, gazing up at one of the glowing, plastic-encased advertisements above the seats facing theirs. Call Doctor Fitz Right Now! His Miraculous Laser Surgery Will Rid You of Acne Forever!

"What's wrong?" Gaia asked.

"Nothing." Mary shrugged. She seemed to be shaking off an unpleasant thought. "Uh, it's just . . . I've been spending a lot of time with Ed lately, you know? And he and I used to be friends. Not *best* friends, but on and off since we were kids." She paused. "Before the accident. It's just weird."

Gaia nodded. Something about Mary's tone struck a strange chord inside her. Had there been some history between her and Ed?

"I mean, we didn't go out or anything," Mary added quickly, answering Gaia's unspoken question. "But we hung out a lot. The thing is, I never feel comfortable around him anymore. And it's all because of that stupid-ass wheelchair. And I know it's ridiculous. It's all in my head. He's still the same person—"

"Don't worry," Gaia soothed. "That kind of thing is natural."

Mary sighed. "Yeah, I guess you're right," she mumbled. "I just wish I had the freaking guts to tell him exactly what was on my mind...."

Gaia kept nodding, but Mary's words floated past her. She was overcome by a sudden and shocking thought: I feel normal. Yes. It was incredible. Here she was, talking to a girl—a *friend*, no less—about another friend. Listening. Offering comfort and advice. The way a normal kid would do. *Her*. Gaia Moore. The freak of nature.

When was the last time she had comforted or advised *anyone*?

Her throat tightened. For a second she was worried she might burst into tears. Jesus. She had to get a grip on herself. This was *not* a big deal. Most people had these kinds of conversations every single day of their lives. But the worst problem with her inability to feel fear was that certain other feelings became exaggerated—probably as some kind of perverse compensation. And in this instance it was gooey sentimentality.

"...boring you to death, aren't I?" Mary was asking.

"Huh?" Gaia shook her head and forced a smile. "No. Sorry. I was just zoning out."

"Well, *I'm* bored to death," Mary said. She raised her eyebrows. "Besides, aren't we forgetting something?"

The train began to slow down.

"What's that?" Gaia asked.

"The *game,* dummy. It's still your turn, right? Why—"

"Seventy-seventh Street!" a voice blared over the loudspeakers.

An impish smile spread across Mary's face. "This is our stop," she said. Suddenly she pointed at Dr. Fitz's miraculous zit-related promises. "I dare you to steal that poster."

The wheels screeched loudly.

Gaia laughed. No way. Mary had to be kidding. It would be impossible to pry that poster from its frame and still exit the train in time. Besides, getting that poster would mean flexing her muscles, which would mean revealing her very abnormal strength to a bunch of strangers—which she hated about as much as she hated being in the presence of Heather Gannis. On the other hand, she always *did* like a challenge. . . .

Impatient-looking commuters gathered by the doors.

"It's now or never," Mary taunted, hopping up from her seat.

The train lurched to a halt.

Gaia's eyes darted around the car. She could do this. She was smiling now, too—smiling in a pulsating, euphoric state of readiness. So Mary thought she could get the best of her, huh? Fat chance.

Her limbs tensed.

Amazing how a simple dare could turn a normal subway exit into a potentially dangerous offense. She had about five seconds. There was only one way to do it....

The doors hissed open.

Before her thoughts were even fully formed, she sprang from her seat and grabbed one of the subway poles, using the momentum to deliver a lightning-fast jump kick. Her leg lashed upward in a blur. The people at the door gasped. The tip of her sneaker struck the plastic with such force and precision that the entire plate instantly shattered.

Whoops.

Senseless vandalism wasn't exactly something Gaia approved of, but this Doctor Fitz sounded like a rip-off artist. Definitely. No way some quack could rid a person of acne forever. She was performing a public service by destroying his false advertising. Well, maybe not. But it was too late to second-guess herself. As she landed, she swiped the crumpled poster from its broken frame—tearing it in half in the process.

Whoops again.

Whatever. Half the poster was good enough. She caught a glimpse of Mary's mile-wide grin. Why wasn't she running? This was no time for horsing around—

"Hey!" a gruff male voice barked. "What the hell do you think you're doing?"

Speak of the devil. A pudgy cop with powdered sugar stains on his blue uniform was at the opposite end of the car. Gaia hadn't even noticed him. But he posed no problem. She was already using the remaining force of her movement to propel her out the door. With her free hand she grabbed Mary's coat sleeve and yanked her out on the platform.

"Freeze!" the cop cried. His face reddened. "You two girls! Don't move—"

The doors slid shut, silencing him.

He was still yelling and gesturing frantically—but Gaia knew there was nothing he could do. The train was pulling from the station. The piercing shriek of the wheels drowned out any other noise. Watching him was like watching a movie with the sound off.

Within seconds he was gone.

"Wow, Gaia!" Mary cried breathlessly. She started cracking up. "Damn! That *ruled!*"

Gaia shook her head. She laughed, too—but she wasn't quite sure how she felt. She glanced around the station. Several onlookers were glaring at them. Bad sign. Time to haul ass out of here before one of them called another cop. She didn't exactly feel like spending the night in a jail cell. Or explaining to George and Ella why she had been arrested . . .

"Come on," she whispered, tugging Mary toward

the exit. She broke into a jog. Mary scrambled after her. Their shoes clattered on the concrete. "We gotta split."

"I think that was the coolest thing I've ever seen," Mary gasped.

The coolest? That wasn't the word Gaia would have used. Silliest was more like it. Or dumbest. But as the two of them hurtled through the turnstiles and dashed upstairs into the wintry Manhattan night, she had to admit something.

The thrill of being bad was undeniable.

She laughed again despite herself. That had been a lot of fun. More fun than she would have expected. Best of all, her real life—the one filled with loneliness and rejection and uncertainty—seemed very, very far away.

THE MOSS GIRL *WAS* A DANGER.

Product Improvement

Loki knew that now. Her danger lay in her stupidity. And apparently, judging from Gaia's latest stunt, that stupidity was contagious.

He scowled as he stood on the corner of Seventy-seventh Street and Lexington Avenue, watching Gaia and her new friend vanish into a mob of pedestrians. This behavior was unacceptable. Absolutely. Gaia's sudden penchant for delinquency called attention to herself. And it had the potential to give her a name and a face among the local authorities—at the very moment he most needed her to be anonymous.

He pulled a cell phone from his overcoat pocket and punched in a series of ten digits, then turned and abruptly strode east toward Third Avenue.

Loki often managed to forget that Gaia was a child. More specifically, that she was a teenager: a swirling vortex of hormonally fueled contradictions. He'd always thought of her as a *product*. He viewed her as the sum total of her unique genetic makeup, of her early environment—but most of all, of her training. Yet it was now clear to him that her training hadn't been rigorous enough. His brother had done a worse job than he'd previously suspected.

But he would show her the value of discipline. She would learn to exercise better judgment. Emotion and insecurity were not supposed to cloud reason. Not in someone of Gaia's ... caliber.

He paused on the corner of Seventy-seventh and Third.

The intersection was very well lit. Christmas lights

in apartment and shop windows cast the street in a multicolored glow. A few passersby jostled him. He surveyed his surroundings just to make sure he wasn't being watched or followed. Security checks were usually unnecessary; still, one could never be too careful. It was a lesson he'd learned from the very beginning. He never forgot it. *His* training had been effective.

He heard the sound of the black Mercedes long before it rolled to a stop beside him. The engine had a distinct timbre, like a person's voice. It was his home away from home. His traveling headquarters.

Under normal circumstances the driver opened the door for him. But he was too cold and too annoyed for formalities. He ducked inside.

The red-haired woman behind the wheel glanced in the rearview mirror.

He slammed the door. The car pulled into the traffic and began to speed downtown.

"Your instincts were right," he told her.

She nodded. "How do you want to proceed?"

"We wait," he stated.

"But . . ." Her brow grew furrowed.

"I want to see how far she can be pushed. I want to know exactly what she's capable of. Peer pressure was a factor I'd never even considered. I'm sure she'll snap out of it."

The woman's lips tightened. "You think so? I think—"

"I don't like your tone," Loki interrupted. "Remember our little talk about focus?"

She didn't reply.

"If she allows herself to be manipulated to the point of real trouble, `we'll have to intervene on her behalf,`" he said, mostly to himself. "We don't have the time to sit back and watch her training deteriorate further. My hope is that she'll come to her senses." He sighed grimly. "I don't want to have to deal with her friend. Her psyche is fragile enough. An accident now will just complicate matters."

Maybe it was time for another whack. Gaia had vowed never to punch her **the christmas** ever again—but **spirit** hey, people broke promises all the time.

TOM MOORE LONGED FOR A PIECE OF PAPER

and a pen. But in Moscow even the most basic luxuries were sometimes impossible to find. The hotel could provide him with vodka, with bad coffee— but on the day before

Next Year in Jerusalem

Christmas, they were out of everything else. Even light-bulbs. His spartan room had a desk, but no desk lamp. And he needed light, too. The days were short at this time of year, and the sun hadn't risen. The only light in the room came from a flickering lamp by his bed, which looked like it had been manufactured during World War II. It was too dim to read or write by.

He shook his head.

Why did they have to assign him to Moscow? Why did they have to torture him?

But the answer was simple enough. He knew the language. He knew the culture. He stretched out on the mattress. It reeked of mothballs.

He closed his eyes and thought of Gaia. He was halfway around the world from her today . . . not too far from where her mother's family had lived for hundreds of years.

The thought made him draw in his breath, wincing involuntarily.

"Katia," he whispered. It had been five years since

her death, but her beautiful face floated in black space before him as clearly as if he were staring at a photograph . . . so much like Gaia's. He shook his head. His lids remained tightly shut. Whenever he came to Russia, Katia's memory clung to him like a shroud, smothering him.

He wondered if Gaia could remember how much Katia had loved her. How she lit up whenever her daughter walked into a room. He wondered if Gaia blamed him for her death—something he'd wondered a million times before. Surely she at least blamed him for disappearing from her life. How could she ever understand he had done it for her safety?

Tom shivered. The hotel room was cold. Outside, a blizzard was raging. It was probably twenty degrees below Fahrenheit out there. But he knew the room wouldn't get any warmer than this. The radiator was turned up as high as it would go, clanking and hissing noisily in the corner. When he'd turned it on, he'd sent cockroaches scurrying.

God, he hated the solitude. He was half tempted to fly to New York immediately, to rush to the Nivens' house and sweep Gaia in his arms—just to have the chance to gaze upon her face . . . but that was impossible. Even watching from afar placed her in jeopardy—

The cell phone at his feet rang. His jaw tightened. Even on Christmas Eve they wouldn't leave him alone. Of course not. He had a job to do. He snatched at the phone, struggling to shake Gaia from his mind.

"Yes?" he croaked.

"Package arriving at eleven hundred, sir," a clipped female voice stated.

"Understood," he replied.

"Sir, it's imperative that we intercept—"

"Understood," Tom repeated again, and disconnected the line.

He forced himself from the mattress. His limbs creaked as he stood in the cold room. He felt a quick flash of anger but thrust it aside. After all his years of service his colleagues and underlings still felt the need to remind him of how "imperative" it was that he perform his duties. He'd personally thwarted over two dozen assassination attempts, bombings, and coups. Yet they always spoke to him as if this were his first mission.

He knew that they were only doing their job, of course. And he knew better than to let his mood affect his work. This was a particularly sensitive matter. The "package" contained plutonium—several million dollars' worth. It was being smuggled from nuclear bases outside Moscow to Afghanistan, then places unknown. If it were to fall into the wrong hands . . .

He knew all of this. He knew that if he failed, there was a chance he could endanger millions of lives. Still, it was amazing how the threat of nuclear terrorism could seem so unimportant in the face of the fact that he couldn't hug his own daughter on Christmas.

The Armed Truce

IT WAS NEARLY ONE O'CLOCK BY THE TIME Gaia tiptoed up to the brownstone on Perry Street.

She prayed that Ella and George were asleep. She had a feeling they weren't. Or at least Ella wasn't. The living-room light was on. It was strange: The emotion Gaia felt as she turned the key in the front door was probably the closest she would ever come to fear. She wasn't scared, of course. But she felt an undeniable reluctance. It was the reluctance of having to occupy the same general space as Ella—and in the worst-case scenario, actually engage in dialogue with her.

As quietly as she could, she pushed open the door.

"Where the hell have you been?"

Gaia bowed her head. The reluctance was justified.

"Look, Ella—"

"You can't go on treating us this way."

Please. Gaia closed the door. Ella was standing in

the middle of the narrow hall. Arms folded across her chest. Nostrils flaring. Wearing that absurd leather miniskirt. Maybe she needed another reminder of how *not* to deal with Gaia. The last time they had gotten into a screaming argument, Gaia had punched her. It had been a reflex; Ella had said something so cruel and horrible that it couldn't be forgiven . . . but at least after that, she had contented herself with being a normal, run-of-the-mill bitch. The blow had frightened her. `Maybe it was time for another whack.` Gaia had vowed never to punch her ever again—but hey, people broke promises all the time.

"Answer me!" Ella barked.

"What's the question?" Gaia asked.

Ella's green eyes narrowed into slits. "Do you really think you can keep on waltzing in and out of here any time of day or night? Do you have any idea what the consequences will be?"

Here we go again, Gaia thought. She slipped out of her coat and hung it in the front hall closet. Ella *did* need another reminder. The Evil Twin was back.

Sometime in the past couple of months Ella had been afflicted with an acute case of multiple-personality disorder. Sometimes she was the surrogate mom. Sometimes she was the doting wife, who pretended to hang on George's every word. (That personality was particularly nauseating.) But other times, like now, she was the Evil Twin. The Wicked Witch of the West Village. A psychopath. Someone out of control.

There was only one reason for the switches, Gaia figured. The woman had a hidden agenda. She was obviously a schemer—and occasionally all the deception took its toll. Maybe she was stealing George's money. It would make sense. There was no way Ella could support herself without him. She was supposed to be this up-and-coming photographer, but Gaia hadn't seen *one* picture she had taken—other than the lame ones in this house. And they certainly weren't of publishable quality. Yes, maybe she was embezzling from George, siphoning his funds into various offshore bank accounts—and then *poof!*—she'd disappear.

Maybe she would even do it sometime soon. George would be a lot better off. Gaia could always hope.

"Don't you have anything to say for yourself?" Ella demanded.

"Like what?"

"Like why you're wandering the streets two days before Christmas?"

"I didn't realize Christmas Eve *Eve* was such a big deal in the Niven household," Gaia replied evenly.

Ella's face darkened. "Well, maybe if you actually spent some *time* here, things would be different," she snapped.

"I spend lots of time here," Gaia muttered. "I probably spend more time here than *you* do. You're the one who's never around."

"That—that . . . that's completely untrue," Ella sputtered.

Gaia suppressed a smile. For once, Ella didn't have a comeback. Of course not. She knew that Gaia was absolutely right.

"You are so goddamn selfish," Ella whispered. "George worries about you so much, and all you do is torture him with your—"

"You know, it's funny, Ella," Gaia interrupted. "You're always yelling at me about how I torture George. But he and I get along fine. When he's actually here."

Ella shook her head. She looked like she could spontaneously combust.

"Besides," Gaia added calmly, "I'm not the one torturing him. You are."

"*Excuse* me?" Ella barked.

"You're hiding something from him," Gaia stated.

Ella's eyes turned to ice. Neither of them moved. It was as if they were on-screen, playing roles in a film that had been paused in the middle of a scene.

Gaia met her gaze unflinchingly.

"You're obviously up to something," she said. "And it's something you don't want George or me to know about. This *act* you play around the house isn't the real you. I don't know what is."

Ella blinked.

The mere batting of eyelashes could betray so much. In that instant Gaia knew that her suspicions were right: Ella *was* a fraud. Something in her face had changed—very subtly and only for the briefest moment. It was as if a mask had slipped. And the expression underneath registered an emotion Gaia had never seen in Ella before. Fear. The fear of being exposed.

"You have no idea what you're talking about," Ella whispered. But the words were flat, unconvincing.

"Look, I don't know what kind of scam you're running," Gaia grumbled. "And to be honest, I really don't care. I just want to be able to cohabitate in peace, all right? We owe George that much at the very least. Even *you* can appreciate that."

In a flash the mask was back in place. Ella took two quick steps forward. "I will *not* be accused of this . . . this *crap* in my own house!" she snarled.

Oooh. Scary. If only Ella knew that she intimidated Gaia about as much as a newborn puppy, they could avoid these cheesy showdowns.

Gaia took two steps forward as well. Their faces were now only inches apart.

"Then let's do something about it," Gaia murmured.

Ella blinked again. "What are you talking about?"

"I propose a bargain," Gaia said. "In keeping with the Christmas spirit. An armed truce. Like what the opposing armies did in World War I."

"Like *who* did?"

Sometimes Gaia had a hard time remembering that age and ignorance were not mutually exclusive. Ella probably didn't know jack shit about World War I. She didn't seem to know anything about history, or literature, or politics—or anything that mattered, really. The sum total of her worldly knowledge was limited to the careers of Mariah Carey and Celine Dion.

"It was Christmas Day in 1916, in France," Gaia explained impatiently. "The Allies and Germans came out of the trenches and played soccer with each other. They acted like friends. Then the next day they went back to their trenches and started killing each other again."

Ella snorted. "You're not making any sense, Gaia."

The woman's thickness was astounding. "Fine." Gaia moaned. "Then let me spell it out for you. On Christmas let's just put all this BS behind us. Let's act civil. I won't tell George you're playing him for a chump, and you won't tell me how to live my life. For twenty-four hours we'll act like a normal family." She flashed a big, fake smile. "Deal?"

Before Ella could respond, Gaia brushed past her and marched up the stairs.

"There's only one problem," Ella called after her. Her voice was mocking.

"What's that?" Gaia asked, rolling her eyes.

"You said an 'armed truce.' But we're not armed. Not unless you're hiding a gun in your room. Which wouldn't surprise me."

Gaia paused on the top step. *Oh, please.* A month ago Ella thought she was hiding drugs. Now guns. What next? Uranium?

"We're armed with our secrets," Gaia said without turning around. "I'd say that's plenty of ammunition, wouldn't you?"

From: gaia13@alloymail.com
To: maryubuggin@alloymail.com
Re: Why Christmas sucks
Time: 1:34 P.M.

Mary—
    You would not believe the shit I had to deal
with this morning. George bought me a pink cash-
mere sweater that could barely fit a five-year-
old. It was nice, but I'm worried he thinks
everyone under forty dresses like his wife.
That's George for you. Sweet but clueless. Then
Ella screamed at me for (a) not buying George a
gift and (b) not being more appreciative. I told
her that I didn't celebrate any Christian holidays, as I worshiped the devil. She didn't find
it funny. So how was your morning? Merry
Christmas, by the way.

From: maryubuggin@alloymail.com
To: gaia13@alloymail.com
Re: Holidays with the ex-coke fiend
Time: 2:34 P.M.

    Get this, Gaia. The only presents I got were
books about the dangers of drugs and alcohol. It
was like a comedy skit or something. *Drinking: A
Love Story*, *Go Ask Alice*, *Smack* . . . My family

must have bought out the Addiction & Recovery
section of the bookstore. It's enough to make a
girl want to freebase. Just kidding. Anyway,
ready for some more truth or dare? How does
tonight sound? I can't wait to get out of this
apartment. Everybody keeps trying to get me to
confess all the terrible things I did and to
talk about my feelings. I feel like I'm on
Oprah.

From: gaia13@alloymail.com
To: smoon@alloymail.com
Re: [no subject]
Time: 3:01 P.M.

    Hey, Sam. I was just writing to say Merry
Christmas. I haven't seen you in a while. By the
way, did we kiss on Thanksgiving, or was that
just in my head? I didn't
<<DELETE>>

From: gaia13@alloymail.com
To: smoon@alloymail.com
Re: [no subject]
Time: 3:03 P.M.

    I love you. I love you. I love you. I
<<DELETE>>

From: gaia13@alloymail.com
To: smoon@alloymail.com
Re: [no subject]
Time: 3:05 P.M.

Hey, Sam. Want to play chess sometime? I think
you need a good ass kicking.

<<DELETE>>

Never before
had she so
longed to be
someone
else, in *déjà*
another
place—a *vu*
million
light-years
from this
living hell.

SAM MOON WAS NOT A SUPERSTITIOUS KIND
of guy. He didn't believe that he
would be cursed for all eternity
if a black cat crossed his path
or that he would be stricken
with cancer if he walked under
a ladder. He didn't believe in
any of that garbage. Life was
not about luck. And contrary to *Forrest Gump,* life was not a box of chocolates, either. Life was a game of chess. Life was about strategy. About seeing the big picture. Fate played no part in it. He'd learned that at a very young age, when he'd first started hustling chess games.

Lightning Strikes

So why had he come back to New York?

Good question. Why had he left his home in Maryland and taken the train all the way back to Manhattan on Christmas night? Because he honestly believed that if Gaia had miraculously appeared in his dorm room on Thanksgiving, there was a chance she might show up on Christmas as well? Was that *really* the reason?

Yes. It was pitiful and wrong and self-defeating, but that *was* reason. He was actually hoping fate would bring him and Gaia together again. In spite of everything. In spite of the fact that she'd stated very clearly that it wasn't going to happen between the two of them.

So he was actually relying on luck. He was relying on her to change her mind. Him. `Mr. Strategy.`

He stood outside the grim dormitory building on West Eleventh Street, gazing up at the rows of darkened windows. He'd told his parents that he had to come back early to make up a physics lab assignment. Which was partially true, in a way. He *did* have to make up a lab assignment. Just not until after New Year's Day.

He should have stayed at home. He'd known that the moment he left, and still he'd come all the way back. His teeth were chattering. A light snow was falling. He was freezing his ass off. There was no *way* Gaia would come here tonight. As the cliché said: Lightning never struck twice in the same place. He could have been sitting by the fireplace right now, sipping a nice hot mug of cider (his mom made *killer* cider), playing chess with Dad. . . .

The old, familiar anger returned.

He *should* be home. He shouldn't be thinking about Gaia at all. She was with her boyfriend. Whoever the hell *he* was. How could she have sent him that e-mail? Because she didn't have the guts to blow him off in person or even over the phone? Yes. She was a coward. A phony. And how could she have been so cold? Couldn't she have said something different? Like: *Dear Sam, Thanks very much for the beautiful chessboard you gave me. I'm sorry I have a boyfriend, but I'll cherish it always. Love, Gaia.*

But no. For all he knew, she had thrown his gift in the garbage. It was a special gift, a *personal* gift, and she didn't care. She didn't care about anything else, either. Like the fact that he'd gotten her to the hospital that Thanksgiving night—the night they kissed. The night he thought they were destined to be together. He'd never experienced a more perfect, magical moment. It was the greatest kiss of his life. . . .

In *his* mind, though. Not hers. A not so subtle distinction.

Clearly she'd been delirious. She probably had no memory of the kiss. No, she probably *did* remember it—but now was so ashamed and humiliated that she was doing her best to avoid him. She probably cringed every time she thought of it. Kicked herself. Made a sour face.

But even as images of Gaia's rejection whirled through his mind, he couldn't help but long for her even *more.* The less she wanted him, the more tantalizing she became.

He shivered again. He'd catch pneumonia if he stayed out here any longer. So he figured he had two options. Option one: He could go upstairs, sit alone in his squalid little dorm room, and stay up all night, thinking about Gaia. Option two: He could go to Heather's house and forget about Gaia altogether.

Gritting his teeth, he turned away from the dorm

and headed in the direction of the subway. He'd cut through the park and get there in no time. Yes. This was the right decision. It was time to finish the process he'd started three weeks ago—the process of making up with Heather. Of recognizing how lucky he was for having such an amazingly beautiful girlfriend. They were finally back on track. They were enjoying each other in a way they hadn't since they first started going out. Besides, the Gannis family would probably *love* to see him on Christmas night. And Heather would be thrilled. Of course.

Unfortunately he happened to catch a glimpse of his distorted reflection in the windshield of a parked car. Shit. He wasn't exactly looking his best. *Would* Heather be happy to see him? His skin was pale. His nose was bright red. His tousled brownish blond hair was matted and covered with snow. And his new wool overcoat made him look like a desperate old pervert. Which in a way, he was—

Wait a second.

He heard laughter. *Familiar* laughter. Coming from the park. He rounded the corner of Eleventh and Fifth, peering through the snowflakes at the Arc de Triomphe. Yes . . . somebody was in there, behind the arch, weaving in and out of the leafless trees. Two people, in fact. Girls. Young. NYU students, maybe, like him. He picked up his pace, crossing Tenth Street in a hurry. His eyes narrowed. One had red hair. . . .

They looked like they were chasing each other.

Another round of giggles echoed off the buildings. Whoever they were, they were having fun. But what were they doing out here on Christmas night?

Actually, the better question was: What was *he* doing out here on Christmas night? Yes. That was the better question. As usual, he was looking for Gaia. But Gaia didn't want his company. No, it was very obvious that she'd found a new scene. A new boyfriend, to be specific. Or an old boyfriend—"from before"—as her e-mail said. Whatever. Either way, she'd moved on. No wonder she hadn't thanked him for his gift. She'd left Sam Moon behind for better things—

"Sam?"

He whirled around. His eyes bulged.

Maybe he *would* start being superstitious.

Tonight might just be his lucky night.

IF HEATHER GANNIS HAD ANY DOUBTS that Sam would be happy to see her, they immediately vanished. His face was lit up like an electronic billboard. Before she knew it, he was sweeping her into an embrace.

No Words Necessary

He practically cut off circulation to the lower half of her body. Well. *This* was a surprise. She wasn't sure if they had officially made up. All their conversations since Thanksgiving had been so . . . *uncertain.*

"What are you doing here?" he cried.

"I called you at home to wish you a merry Christmas," she said. She took a deep breath and gently extricated herself from Sam's arms, brushing a few strands of long, dark hair out of her eyes. "Your parents told me that you came back early. I figured you'd be here. I thought I'd surprise you."

"I'm glad you did," he murmured.

She stared into his eyes. Ever since their troubles started, it seemed the best response she could get out of him was a strained smile and faraway look. But now she saw something new. Or something old, really. Focus. He was entirely *here*. With her. In the moment. Just like when they first started going out all those months ago. It had been so long since he'd been able to gaze at her the way he was gazing at her now. Even when they had made love that one time, he'd seemed distant—as if his brain were disconnected and his body was on autopilot. And then when Gaia Moore walked in on them, it was clear that his mind *had* been elsewhere.

But maybe he had finally gotten over her. The psycho. The bitch who had single-handedly nearly destroyed Heather's life. Of course, there was no point in thinking about Gaia right now. Wherever she was, she wasn't with them—and that was good enough.

"So what are you doing out here in the cold?" she asked. "It's freezing."

"Going to look for you," he answered.

"Well, you found me," she whispered. He couldn't have given her a better reply if she had scripted it herself. Her pulse picked up a beat. She saw something else in his eyes, too. Desire. Yes. It had been a *very* long time since she'd seen that. For all of Heather's popularity and good looks, for all of her supposed confidence and charm, she knew she was very insecure at heart. A strange pain stirred in her stomach. That was probably why she'd allowed herself to end up in bed with Charlie Salita a couple of weeks ago. But there was no point in thinking about *him,* either. Or the fact that she still didn't know if he'd raped her. . . .

Sam bit his lip. "Heather, I—"

"Let's not talk," she interrupted. Her voice was barely a whisper. "Let's just be together. We don't need to say anything. Not yet, anyway."

He nodded.

Without a word, he took her hand and led her back down Fifth Avenue to his dormitory.

Training School for Badasses

Mary's lungs were about to explode. There was no way she could keep chasing that girl. For one thing, Gaia was in superhuman shape. For another, Mary's own body was still rebounding from years of drug abuse. She wasn't exactly in marathon condition.

"What's the matter?" Gaia taunted from the end of the block. "I'm not too fast for you, am I? Come on. How badly do you want your wallet back?"

Go ahead and keep it, Mary wanted to answer. But all that came out of her mouth was a pathetic little gasp. She leaned against a lamppost, struggling to catch her breath. She sucked in huge gulps of freezing air. It felt like ice was tearing into her chest. She couldn't get enough oxygen. Whoa. She was actually kind of dizzy. Her head throbbed. Purplish dots swam before her eyes.

"Mary?" Gaia called. Her tone suddenly became serious. "Are you all right?"

Mary shook her head. No. *All right* would not be the phrase she'd use to describe herself right now. But in spite of the fact that she was mildly afraid of dropping dead, she couldn't help but feel embarrassed.

This was so lame. Here she was, a seventeen-year-old girl, in the prime of her life—and she was legitimately worried about heart failure. Christ. But that was what she deserved, she supposed. It was amazing she *hadn't* dropped dead yet.

On the plus side, all the running around had taken her mind off Skizz. Because there was a very good chance Skizz would be lurking around the shadows here somewhere, trying to sell his product. Or looking for her.

Gaia ran back down the street. Her face was creased with concern. "Hey," she called. "What's the matter?"

"Nothing, nothing," Mary mumbled. Gradually her dizziness faded. Her rattling pulse slowed. She straightened, using the metal pole to hoist herself up. "It's just . . . ah, I guess I'm kind of winded. That's all. It'll pass."

"Are you sure?" Gaia asked, peering into Mary's face.

Mary nodded. She forced herself to forget about Skizz. "You know, I should have known better than to dare you to steal something valuable of mine," she muttered with a smirk. "It figures you'd be a great pickpocket."

Gaia raised her eyebrows, pretending to be offended. "Oh, yeah? Why's that?"

"It just goes along with your other talents," Mary

said. Her breathing finally evened. "Did you, like, go to some special training school for badasses when you were a kid?"

"Hey," Gaia protested, wagging a finger at her. "No truths, remember?"

Mary rolled her eyes. "But that's just a question. It's not part of the—"

"Uh-uh," Gaia interrupted. "Anyway, you can't ask me anything. It's your turn." She handed Mary's wallet back to her. "So what'll it be? Truth or dare?"

"Well, I'm way too spent for a dare," Mary mumbled, shoving her wallet back into her inside coat pocket. How *had* Gaia managed to swipe it, anyway? But there was no point in asking herself that question. Gaia would never tell her. "I think you're gonna have to truth me."

Gaia smiled. Her eyes sparkled in the pale light of the streetlamp. She glanced around the deserted street, tapping a gloved finger against her chin. "Hmmm. Let's see. . . . Let's see. . . . Okay, I got one. Truth: What's the worst-possible thing you could dare me to do?"

Mary had to laugh. "You know, I'm starting to worry about you," she said. "Thanks to all the books I got for Christmas, I'm an expert at recognizing the symptoms of addiction. And you, my friend, are definitely a dare addict."

"Who, *me?*" Gaia asked sarcastically. She shook her head. "Mary, that's not it at all. It's just that it's about minus fourteen degrees out here with the windchill factor, and I want to keep moving. Truths are way too inactive." She hopped up and down and rubbed the sleeves of her coat for dramatic effect. "So? What is it?"

"What's what?"

"What's the worst-possible thing you can dare me to do?" Gaia asked impatiently.

Mary thought for a moment. Now that her cardiovascular system had reached a relative state of normalcy again, she was beginning to realize that Gaia was right: It *was* freezing out here. Whatever this dare was, it would have to involve warmth. And it would have to involve Mary, too. And maybe some more layers of clothing . . .

Aha. Yes. There was a simple way to satisfy all three needs.

"You know, it occurs to me that a lot of NYU students live around here," Mary said, glancing up at the row houses on MacDougal Street. "And I bet they're all gone for the holidays. So here it is. I dare you to sneak into somebody's room and steal all their clothes."

Gaia pursed her lips. "Mary," she said with a groan. "Come on. We shouldn't steal from people, you know? I feel bad enough about the subway thing—"

"You can return the clothes tomorrow," Mary interrupted. "They'll never know the difference. And I'll come with you. That way if we get caught, we'll both share the blame."

"Yeah, but . . ." Gaia still didn't look convinced.

"Hey," Mary said, shrugging nonchalantly. "You asked me what the worst dare is I could think of, and that's it. Go and steal somebody's clothes. And it's not even that bad. I mean, I'm coming with you." She grinned. "Now, does this mean the great Gaia Moore is wimping out on me? Does this mean I won the game?"

"You wish," Gaia said. She started smiling again, too. "All right. So which dorm?"

"Any one you want," Mary said. "There's a bunch over on Eleventh Street."

All at once Gaia's smile vanished.

"What is it?" Mary asked.

"Uh . . . nothing. I was just thinking that Sam Moon lives around here. He . . . uh, he lives on that block. I could take *his* stuff."

Mary hesitated. "Wait a sec. This wouldn't be an excuse to piss Heather off, would it?"

Gaia laughed grimly and shook her head.

"Well, okay," Mary answered uncertainly. She studied Gaia's face. Something strange was going on here. For the first time ever, Gaia did not look supremely confident. No. She looked . . . well, *sad*. She was clearly hiding something. Not that this was anything new. But usually when somebody mentioned Heather's name, Gaia became *angry*—not sad. So . . . this wasn't about Heather. This was about Sam. There obviously *was* some kind of history between Sam and Gaia.

So . . . maybe this would be a good way to find out what was going on. Maybe Mary could actually pry a truth out of Gaia without having to actually truth her. It was worth a shot.

"Ready?" Gaia asked.

"I'm ready if you are," Mary said.

GAIA STILL WASN'T SURE EXACTLY *WHY* she'd decided to break into Sam's dorm. It was an undeniably stupid thing to do. But in a crazy way, she was actually sort of hoping that Sam would be there. Because then she'd finally get the answer to the question that had been gnawing at her sanity for a month: *Did we kiss or not?*

The Answer

And then she'd be able to get on with her life. For better or for worse.

Getting past the security guard was no problem at all. Gaia had come up with a foolproof system for sneaking into Sam's dorm on Thanksgiving night. She'd tripped the guard's car alarm. The piercing siren was the only thing that could get the guy to leave his post. He always parked his car right outside the building—probably so he could keep an eye on it.

Sure enough, Gaia saw the car the instant she and Mary turned off Fifth Avenue onto West Eleventh Street. It was a fairly nondescript American sedan— but the telltale sign was its ridiculous vanity plate: RANGERFAN.

Why was it that all macho meatheads had sports-related vanity plates?

"Stay back a sec," she instructed Mary.

Mary paused on the sidewalk. Gaia crept along the side of the building and peered around the corner into the entranceway. There the guard was, sitting in the lobby, his pudgy face lit up with a bluish glow from the flickering light of the TV screen. She almost felt bad for him. Nobody should have to work on Christmas night. It was just too depressing.

Oh, well. At least she would liven up his shift.

Mary tiptoed up behind her. "What's going on?" she whispered.

"We gotta get past the guard," Gaia whispered back.

Ducking down, she scoured the ground for something to throw at the car. . . . *Bingo*. There was an empty forty-ounce bottle of malt liquor near the curb. She scuttled over and grabbed it, then ran back to Mary.

"What are you gonna do?" Mary asked. Her forehead was wrinkled, but she was smiling. "You aren't gonna crack that over his head, are you?"

"Please," Gaia moaned with a giggle. "I'm not into victimization, remember? All you have to do is follow me into the building as fast as you can. Ready?"

"Uh . . . I guess so. . . ."

Gaia hurled the bottle directly at the license plate. It spun end over end and smashed into the car just over the rear fender, exploding in a loud shatter. Almost instantaneously the car alarm erupted. The sound of the siren tore through the icy night.

"Jesus!" Mary hissed. She bit her lip, trying to keep from laughing.

Three seconds later the guard came bounding out the door.

So predictable. Like clockwork. He ran right up to the rear fender and scowled at it, then glanced out onto the street—in the opposite direction of Gaia and Mary. Perfect. Gaia tapped Mary's shoulder and bolted into the lobby. The blast of heated, indoor air washed over her like an invisible tidal wave—sending much needed relief to her chilled bones. Mary followed close on her heels. Gaia pulled her into the stairwell.

"What floor?" Mary whispered.

"Fourth."

Excitement fizzed in Gaia's veins as she hurried up the flights of stairs. She was barely conscious of Mary's wheezing behind her. A dozen disjointed memories swirled through her mind: sneaking into Sam's room and taking a shower . . . the time she walked in on him and Heather in bed . . . the dream of that wonderful kiss and his words in her ear: "*I love you*" . . . she shook her head. Goose bumps rose on her arms.

"This is it?" Mary whispered when they reached the fourth-floor landing.

Gaia nodded.

"Good," Mary said. "Because I'm about to pass out again."

As quietly as she could, Gaia crept into the hall outside Sam's suite—then stopped in her tracks. The door was open. Was somebody there?

"What is it?" Mary asked.

Gaia shook her head. The faintest scrap of conversation drifted past her ears. It was completely unintelligible; she couldn't even tell if it was a boy or girl—but *somebody* was there. She took another two steps forward—

"My God, Sam," a girl's voice whispered. "That was incredible. . . ."

Oh, no. Not her.

Gaia's knees turned to jelly. The sound of that voice was like a sword, shredding her insides. Never before had she so longed to be someone else, in another place—a million light-years from this living hell.

The voice belonged to Heather Gannis.

Gaia was sure of it. There was no doubt in her

mind. And in that instant she had her answer. Her throat tightened. Sam *hadn't* kissed her that night. He might have brought her to the hospital; he might have even bundled her up in his clothes—but that was it. Why had she come here? It was like déjà vu. She had walked in on the boy she loved most in the arms of the girl she hated most. She didn't even have to *see* them to know that they were together in bed. No, Heather's few husky words painted a `perfectly clear picture`. And there was nothing Gaia could do to stop them. Sam Moon didn't love her. He loved Heather Gannis. Period.

"Gaia?" Mary whispered.

She turned around, her lips trembling.

Mary was still standing by the stairwell door. She looked very afraid.

"I don't think I can do this," Gaia choked out. "I think I have to get out of here. . . ."

She was barely aware of Mary's leading her back down the stairs and into the freezing night. It was hard to see through the tears.

Skizz chuckled.
His laugh was
very easygoing
and friendly—
which

bad

somehow only

debts

made it
more terrifying.
"Then we have a
problem," he
said.

IF MARY COULD COUNT ON *ONE* THING

Call Number One . . .

in life, it was that Gaia Moore would end up okay. Gaia Moore would always find a way to survive, no matter how bad things got. So there was no point in worrying. Right?

Wrong, a silent voice answered.

In the old days, Mary used to tune out that voice by doing a quick blast of coke. She shook her head. Bad to think of coke. Very bad. She paced the floor of her vast bedroom, kicking through the clothes that were strewn everywhere. Amazing how depressing the place looked when she wasn't high. Even after a month of sobriety, she still hadn't managed to clean it. But the mess used to be a comfort; she felt like she could hide in it—as if the heaps of dirty laundry were actually enchanted mountains in a magical, secret world. When she locked the doors and sliced out a couple of lines in the mirror, everything around her became transformed. . . .

"Stop thinking about drugs!" she hissed out loud.

She glanced at the clock on her desk. It was already past six. A whole day had come and gone—and she still had heard no word from Gaia. Nobody had picked up at Gaia's house when Mary had tried to call there, either. But it wasn't as if they had made definite plans or anything. After they bolted from that dorm last night, Gaia had just kept on running. She hardly even said good-bye. She didn't even look back. For all Mary knew, Gaia had gone upstate on some foster family outing.

Yeah. Sure.

A person didn't have to spend a lot of time with Gaia Moore to know that foster family outings played no role in her life.

But at the very least, Mary had made an important discovery last night. There definitely *was* some history between Gaia and Sam Moon—

The phone on her desk rang.

Finally, she thought. She ran over to grab it—but unfortunately, there was no place for her to sit. All of those stupid Christmas books were stacked on her desk chair. Jesus. She was definitely going to have to trade them in for some *real* gifts. With an impatient swat, she shoved them onto the floor, then snatched up the phone and plopped down into the soft, cushiony seat.

"Hello?"

"I want my five hundred dollars, bitch."

The blood drained from Mary's face. It wasn't Gaia.

"S-S-Skizz?" she stuttered.

"Hello?" her mom answered on another phone.

Shit. "I got it, Mom," she said quickly. "I got it—"

"Okay, dear." Her tone was cheerful. "Dinner will be ready in five minutes, so keep it short, okay—"

"I *got* it," she hissed.

There was a fumbling click.

"Aw," Skizz said, his voice gravelly. "Ain't that sweet? Well, don't worry, *dear*. You're gonna make dinner. We ain't got much to talk about."

Mary's breath started coming fast. "How did you get this number?" she whispered.

Skizz started cracking up. "Damn, girl, you musta been more messed up than I thought. You don't remember giving it to me?"

No, she didn't. Then again, she wouldn't be surprised if Skizz were lying right now. That was one of the many two-sided problems with drugs: you did things you couldn't remember, but you also hung out with con artists who made up lies about you. And since your brain was fried most of the time, you could never provide any evidence to contradict those lies. You never knew the truth. But it was always safe to assume the worst.

"Well, that's okay," Skizz went on. "I won't take it personally. All I want is my money. Then you won't have to worry about me calling you again. Ever."

Mary swallowed. Her eyes kept darting to the door. What if her mother decided to come in right now? She should have locked it; but then, she wasn't *allowed* to lock it anymore. That was one of the conditions of her cleanup program.

"I don't have your money," Mary said finally.

Skizz chuckled. His laugh was very easygoing and friendly—which somehow only made it more terrifying. "Then we have a problem," he said.

"Look, just give me a couple of weeks to get it together, all right?" Mary whispered frantically. She could feel herself starting to panic. "I swear to God, I'll get it to you. It's just . . . I don't—I mean, my family will be suspicious if I start taking money out of the bank in huge amounts, so—"

"I don't need your life story, sugar," he interrupted coldly. "I just need that five hundred bucks."

She shook her head. "I . . . I . . ."

"Don't think you can hide. I know where to find you. I can come up to that swanky Park Avenue apartment, or I can wait for you downtown. Makes no difference to me. And this time if that psycho blond bitch tries anything, I'll be ready."

"Don't touch her," Mary whispered instinctively. God, why did he have to drag Gaia into this mess? Well, actually, she knew the reason. Gaia had kicked the shit out of him once already. His reputation would be severely damaged if rival dealers found out he'd been beaten up by a girl—*twice*.

He laughed again. "Fine. You got twenty-four hours. You know where to find me. If you don't, I'm coming to find *you*."

Mary opened her mouth to plead with him one last time. But the line was already dead.

SAM FULLY EXPECTED THE RAGING BATTLE

in his head to be over. He'd made his decision. Or rather, *Heather* had made his decision for him. She'd been incredible. Like some kind of wild goddess. A month

Call Number Two . . .

on the rocks did wonders for a relationship. Especially the physical part. There was no way anybody could top the way Heather made him feel last night. None. He still couldn't quite believe it. Even in memory it seemed more like a crazy, erotic dream than reality.

So why was he miserable?

Well, for one thing, he was stuck in his dorm room the day after Christmas. Aside from him and the security guard, the entire place was deserted. And he couldn't go to Heather's because she was up visiting relatives in Connecticut. Loneliness always made a person depressed. Then there was the fact that his dorm room had no windows and was the size of a prison cell—and was seriously beginning to reek. He hadn't changed his sheets since . . . well, it was best not to think about that.

But he was lying to himself. He knew it. He was just making up reasons to be bummed out. Anything to prevent him from seeing the truth.

The battle wasn't over.

He stared at the phone, half buried under a pile of papers next to his computer. He could just call her. Right now. He could at least find out if she'd kept the chessboard. If she hadn't thrown it out, then he would finally know for sure if it was even worth this agony.

She doesn't give a shit about the stupid chessboard, you idiot.

Whatever. Impulsively he grabbed the phone and punched in Gaia's number, sending the papers flying.

"Hello?" a woman answered after two rings.

"Um . . . hi." Sam cleared his throat. It must have been her foster mom. He suddenly found his palms were moist. Maybe he should have waited a little longer and planned exactly what he was going to say. "Is Gaia there, please?"

"May I ask who's calling?"

"This is, uh . . . this is Sam," he said.

"Oh, hi." Her voice suddenly brightened. "I'm Ella."

"Uh . . . hi," he answered awkwardly. Why did she sound so pleased to talk to him? She didn't even *know* him. His mouth was dry. "How are you?"

"Very well, thanks. And you, Sam?"

Was it his imagination, or was her tone a little . . . flirtatious? She was speaking very quietly and intimately. It kind of gave him the creeps.

"I'm fine," he said. "So . . ."

"I'm sorry, sweetie. Gaia isn't here right now."

He bit his lip. "Do you know where she is?"

Ella sighed. "With that boyfriend of hers, I imagine."

Snap. Ka-boom. `Thermonuclear detonation.` Mushroom cloud. A red haze filled Sam's brain. Nervousness turned to rage. "Who is this guy, anyway?" he found himself demanding.

"I don't know. But whoever he is, I'm sure he isn't half as cute as you." She sighed again. "Gaia's not known for her judgment, though."

No. She sure as hell wasn't. And Sam was going to give her a piece of his—

Hold on. Did Gaia's foster mom just call him *cute?* Yeah. She did. But how could she even know if he was cute or not? She'd never even *seen* him. Blood rushed to his face. This was more than creepy. . . .

"Sam? Are you there?"

"Uh . . . yeah—yeah," he stammered clumsily. "Listen, can I ask you something?"

"Anything," she answered in a sultry whisper.

His skin was starting to crawl. "I just want to know if you've ever seen her with, um, a new chessboard," he said. "You know, playing chess."

"I sure haven't. I think she plays chess in the park—"

"Thanks," he cut in, slamming the phone down on the hook.

Well. There it was. Not a lot of gray area. Nope. Gaia had thrown away the gift.

Gaia was out of the picture.

So. It was probably about time to give his amazingly hot, ready-and-willing girlfriend a call in Connecticut.

Call Number Three . . .

"ELLA?" GAIA YELLED FROM THE TOP OF the stairs. "Did somebody just try to call me?"

Gaia could have sworn she'd heard the phone ring while she was in the shower. She wasn't the type to imagine things. Well, she *had* imagined that Sam had kissed her—but that was due to a traumatic head injury. She tightened the towel around her body and ran a hand through her soaking hair.

"Ella!" she shouted. "Are you—"

"Quiet!" Ella barked. She stamped loudly up the

stairs to the third-floor landing and glared up at Gaia. "We have neighbors."

Then why are you yelling? Gaia wondered, but she kept a lid on her anger. She wasn't in the mood for a fight right now. "Sorry," she murmured with as much politeness as she could manage. "I was just wondering if that call was for me."

Ella raised her eyebrows. "Why? Are you expecting to hear from someone?"

Gaia's jaw tightened. Asking meddling, inappropriate questions was Ella's specialty. She'd probably guessed correctly that Gaia *was* hoping to hear from someone. Namely Sam—so he could explain why the hell he went back to his heinous girlfriend after what had happened between him and Gaia . . . whatever it was.

She drew in a sharp breath. She would *not* think about Sam. Never again. It was her New Year's resolution, and it was coming a little early. Besides, Gaia didn't want to hear from Sam, anyway. She wanted to hear from Mary, so she could have the opportunity to explain why she had freakishly bolted from Sam's dorm the night before. But Ella had been online half the day. And Gaia had been too embarrassed to call Mary herself. She just hoped Mary wasn't mad.

"And would you please put something on your feet?" Ella demanded in the silence. "You're dripping all over the place. Water is bad for the carpet."

Unbelievable. But Gaia simply plastered a big, fake smile on her face. Sometimes the best offense was passive resistance. Ella always got the most frustrated when Gaia refused to engage in an argument.

"No problem," Gaia said sweetly. "I'll put something on my feet just as soon as you answer my question. Was that call for me?"

Ella blinked. "No. It wasn't." She turned and marched back down the stairs.

Gaia rolled her eyes. Obviously it *was*. Good thing Ella Niven was a wanna-be photographer and not a covert agent, like her husband. She was probably the worst liar Gaia had ever met. And it wasn't a good quality for somebody who was trying to play her husband for a chump, either.

It was strange, though. There was no possible reason Ella could have for preventing Gaia from getting phone calls. Then again, Ella wasn't famous for making sense.

Gaia trudged into her bedroom (not that she really thought of it as *hers;* it was just the room she temporarily inhabited), picked up the phone on the desk, and dialed *69.

But instead of ringing, she heard three painfully loud and atonal beeps—the sound of a nonworking or disconnected number.

"We're sorry," a computerized female voice

answered. "At your request, this feature has been deactivated. If you wish to have it—"

Gaia hung up the phone. She scowled in bewilderment. Why the hell would George and Ella deactivate the *69 feature? Why would anyone . . .

CIA, Gaia suddenly realized. George probably wanted to make sure that none of the incoming calls from the Agency could be traced—for security purposes. Now that she thought about it, her father had done the same thing. Deactivating the *69 feature was probably company policy. Wonderful. Just her luck. For all Gaia knew, that could have been Sam, calling to confess his love for her. She laughed miserably. Yeah. Chances of that were approximately one in four zillion.

But it wasn't as if she had to launch a massive investigation. Only two people in the world would possibly call her. Mary or Ed. She decided to try Mary first.

"Hello?" Mary's mom answered after two rings.

"Hi, Mrs. Moss," Gaia said. She realized she felt a little funny about calling—and not only because she had some explaining to do to Mary. No, it was also because the last time she'd spoken with Mary's mother had been Thanksgiving night: the very same night Gaia had discovered Mary hunched over a pile of cocaine in her room and bolted from the scene. She wondered for a moment if Mrs. Moss thought that *she* did cocaine, too. "It's Gaia Moore. Is Mary around?"

"Oh, hi, dear!" Mrs. Moss exclaimed. "She's in the middle of dinner. I'll have her call you as soon as she's finished."

"Uh . . . thanks," Gaia murmured. She breathed a little sigh of relief. "I'll be home all night."

"You know, Gaia, I never had the opportunity to thank you," Mrs. Moss said. "If it weren't for you, Mary never would have gotten on the track she is now. We owe you."

Gaia's face grew hot. She'd never been good at accepting compliments—mostly because she rarely got them, except from old drunks who liked her blond hair. "No . . . it was, it's uh, nothing," she mumbled clumsily.

"If there's anything we can do for you, just let us know," Mrs. Moss said.

"That's really nice of you. But I'm fine. Thanks. Bye." Before Mrs. Moss could get another word in, Gaia quickly hung up the phone. Jesus. She had nothing to do with Mary's sobriety. *Mary* did. She hated the idea of somebody's being indebted to her—almost as much as she hated the idea of being indebted to somebody else. Debts made it very hard to pick up and leave at a moment's notice. That was part of the reason she'd been so reluctant to be friends with Mary in the first place. Ed too, for that matter.

She sighed. Clearly Mary hadn't called; she was

eating. That left Ed. But after two rings the answering machine picked up at his apartment. "Hello, you've reached the Fargo residence. . . ."

She dropped the phone down on the hook. So Ed wasn't home, either.

Who the hell had called her, anyway? Was Ella telling the truth? Was the call really for somebody else?

Gaia shook her head. No. The idea of Ella's being honest was far too disturbing.

ELLA WAS JUST BEGINNING TO FEEL relaxed when she felt the silent buzz of the cellular in the front pocket of her sweater. Her face twisted in a scowl. Loki always picked the worst times to call. She could never enjoy a single moment's peace.

Call Number Four . . .

Oh, well. She stood and grabbed her leather coat from the hall closet. For an instant her gaze fell on a small red package—tucked back amidst a bunch of junk that Gaia would never think to search. Sam's gift. Ella allowed herself a little smile. Poor, poor Gaia. The girl would never know just how much the boy cared for her. It was Ella's secret. And she had to be careful. If Loki found out that Ella was interfering so dramatically in Gaia's personal affairs, she would probably wind up at the bottom of the East River.

But a woman needed her diversions.

Ella stepped quickly out into the brisk December night and fished the cellular phone out of her pocket. She walked west on Perry Street toward the Hudson. Christ, it was freezing. Her nose burned in the biting wind. She probably could have stayed at home, but Loki insisted that she never communicate with him in the Niven household. He was obsessive about security. Too obsessive. But she couldn't afford to take chances. He very well may have been watching her right at this moment.

"Yes?" she answered.

"The Moss problem may solve itself," Loki stated.

Ella paused, smiling confusedly. She glanced up and down the block just to make sure she was alone. "How's that?"

"She owes money to a drug dealer. He's nothing more than a street thug, but he's dangerous. He's given her an ultimatum. Twenty-four hours."

Ella's smile widened. She began walking again, rounding the corner onto West Fourth Street to escape the wind. "What should we do?"

"Nothing. See how it plays. I'll contact you later.

Keep an eye on Gaia, though. Make sure she doesn't get involved."

"Right." Ella clicked the phone shut and shoved it back into her pocket. Poor, poor Gaia indeed. So there was a good chance she would lose her boyfriend *and* her best friend. All within the space of a few days. It was turning out to be a merry Christmas after all.

Top Ten Reasons I Should Avoid Gaia Moore Like the Plague and Never Speak to Her Again

1. She nearly got me killed by a bunch of skinheads.
2. She nearly got me killed by a serial killer.
3. She pisses me off.
4. She's in love with Sam Moon.
5. She's involved with something really bad and mysterious that she can't talk about.
6. This bad and mysterious thing will probably get her killed.
7. This bad and mysterious thing will probably get me killed, too, if I keep hanging out with her.
8. She has no redeeming social skills.
9. Every time I think about her, I get a headache.
10. I'm in a wheelchair, and she isn't.

Top 10 Reasons I Should Keep Hanging Out with Her

1. She does a kick-ass imitation of that little kid from *The Sixth Sense*.

    That's about it. Oh, yeah. I'm also in love with her. Does that count?

He'd
learned a
long time
ago that it
was **bearded**
wise to be **clones**
paranoid
when hanging
out with
Gaia.

ED WASN'T SURE EXACTLY WHAT DROVE
him to accept Gaia's invitation
and meet her and Mary in
Washington Square Park that
night. He sure as hell wasn't
psyched to play more truth or
dare. No, he figured there were
probably two reasons—a desper-

The New Gaia

ate need to be in Gaia's presence and utter boredom.
Pretty much the usual.

Plus he had been spending *way* too much time with
his family the past few days. Christmas was already
forty-eight hours behind him, and his parents were still
planning holiday events—as if dragging him to New
Jersey yesterday to visit his grandparents wasn't torture
enough. For some reason, his mom and dad really
seemed to believe that there were actually twelve days
of Christmas—and each of those days required some
kind of painfully awkward family gathering.

At least he'd escaped for a while. And it was a little
warmer, which probably explained why the park was
so crowded at this late hour. Well, that and the fact
that all the I'm-too-hip-for-words NYU students were
coming back early from Christmas break so they could
be in the city for New Year's Eve. Ed snickered to himself as he entered from the southeast. He almost
felt sorry for these people—the kids on the
benches in their leather jackets and baggy jeans,

huddled around each other in tight circles for warmth. All of them wanted to pretend that they were native New Yorkers. But no amount of body piercing could alter the fact that most of them grew up in lame states like Iowa or Kansas or Montana.

He rolled slowly along the brightly lit pathway, scanning for signs of Gaia. There was a lot of action at the chess tables, but he couldn't see—

"Yo! Ed! Over here!"

There she was—standing by the fountain with Mary, waving furiously. God, the more those two hung out together, the more they started to dress like twins. Gaia had bought the same black wool hat as Mary— and Mary had bought Gaia's overcoat. Their outfits were practically identical. It was kind of scary.

But what was even scarier was that Gaia was smiling.

This had been happening a lot lately. It was a fairly strange development, as far as Ed was concerned. Before she'd met Mary, her facial expressions were pretty much limited to various forms of anger. Ed had gotten used to it. He'd come to *expect* it. The fearsome, unsmiling Gaia was the one he had fallen for. But Mary seemed to have some kind of bizarre nor-malizing effect on her, in a way that he never had. The new Gaia didn't seem to take life as seriously. The new Gaia acted like any other run-of-the-mill seventeen-year-old. . . .

He shook his head. Maybe Gaia was just smiling

because she was psyched to see him. Or she was full of Christmas cheer. He should be happy that *she* was happy. So why wasn't he?

"What's up, guys?" he called as he rolled toward them. "You thinking of auditioning for a Doublemint commercial?"

Gaia smirked. "Very funny."

"Hey, my grandma bought me this coat for Christmas," Mary said. "It was out of my hands. I swear."

Ed shook his head, slowing to a stop in front of them. "Yeah, sure," he said with a lopsided grin. "Grandmothers never buy anything that cool. Trust me. I know. Mine gave me a pair of polyester 'slacks.'" He made little quotation marks in the air with his fingers. "Her word, not mine."

Mary laughed. "So how was Christmas, anyway, Fargo?"

"Boring," he grumbled. "Why do you think I came out here to hang with you guys?"

"Because you want to be seen in public with two amazingly hot chicks," Mary joked.

Ed flashed a fake smile. *Actually, yes,* he thought. *You're right.* The really sad thing was that Mary had no idea how beautiful she was. And neither did Gaia. They suffered from the opposite problem that Heather did. *She* thought she was God's gift to men. How could certain people be so insightful about others and yet so utterly stupid about themselves?

"So do you feel like getting back in the action?" Gaia asked, rubbing her gloved palms together. "You've got a lot of turns to make up. We've been on a pretty wild ride so far."

"I'm sure you have," he mumbled.

"Let's get out of the park, though," Mary said quickly. "Let's go someplace we hardly ever go. Like Chinatown or something."

Ed stared at her, his brow furrowing. Mary seemed a little jumpy again. Her eyes kept flitting from one group of people to the next. And she couldn't stand still. She kept shifting her weight from one foot to the other.

"We just got here," Gaia pointed out.

"Yeah, but . . . I—I don't know," she stammered distractedly. "It's just kind of dull."

"What's the matter?" Ed asked.

Mary shook her head—a little too emphatically. "Nothing," she said.

Ed exchanged a quick glance with Gaia. She shrugged.

"We can split," Gaia said. "Whatever. I've never been to Chinatown before."

Before Gaia had even finished, Mary was already hurrying toward the north exit, straight under the arch. Gaia jogged after her.

Ed frowned. Okay. Mary was freaking out about

something. He was not imagining this. He followed them slowly, peering to his left into a darkened clump of trees. Maybe she had seen an ex-boyfriend, or—

Him.

Ed's chair jerked to a stop. There was a guy. A fat guy with a beard—standing under a tree, hidden in the shadows not thirty feet away. He was staring directly at Gaia and Mary. Ed shivered. The night didn't seem as pleasant as it had before. He was freezing, in fact. Cold air nipped at his nose and ears. That guy looked familiar. Ed had definitely seen him around the park before. In fact . . . yeah, *he* was the guy who'd been staring at Mary the other day. So he must have been the reason she was freaking out. Ed's gaze flashed back to the two girls. They vanished briefly behind the right side of the Arc de Triomphe. He turned back. . . .

The guy was gone.

For a few moments Ed craned his neck, trying to spot him—but all he saw were tree branches, swaying in the winter wind under the ghostly lights of the park. Had the guy figured out that Ed had noticed him? More important, was he following Mary? Or Gaia? That was a distinct possibility. In fact, it was a *probability*. He'd learned a long time ago that it was wise to be paranoid when hanging out with Gaia. Any real danger always ended up exceeding his wildest fears, anyway.

"Hey, Ed!" Gaia called. "Are you coming or what?"

His head whipped around. Gaia and Mary were already halfway down the block, heading east. His eyes darted around the street on the other side of the park fence. The guy was nowhere to be found. As quickly as he could, Ed sped out of the park, nearly tipping as he whipped through the arch and around the corner onto the sidewalk.

"Jesus." Gaia looked at Mary, frowning. "Are you all right?"

"Did you see something, Mary?" he interrupted, skidding to a halt beside them. His icy gasps filled the air.

Mary and Gaia exchanged a quick glance.

"What do you mean?" Mary asked. Her forehead wrinkled.

"A guy," Ed whispered. He glanced back over his shoulder. But the street was deserted. "A guy with a beard. A long beard."

Mary's face seemed to go blank. She blinked several times.

"What?" Gaia demanded.

Ed held his breath, waiting.

"Uh . . . nothing," Mary said. Her voice was subdued. She shook her head and cast a brief glance back at the park. "No. I didn't see a guy with a long beard."

"Do you *know* a guy with a long beard?" Ed asked.

Mary didn't say anything. All at once Gaia started laughing.

105

Ed grimaced. "You mind telling me what's so funny?"

"Nothing," she muttered, shaking her head. She pulled her hat down tightly over her tangled mop of blond hair. "I just didn't know that you had such strong feelings against guys with beards."

"Uh . . . we should go," Mary said. She turned back down the block and started walking east again. "It's too cold to be standing still."

Ed glared at Gaia. Obviously Mary knew this guy—whoever he was. Obviously she was scared of him. So why the hell was Gaia still smiling? Why was she turning this into a joke?

"*What?*" Gaia asked defensively.

"Excuse me for being uptight, but I just get a little anxious when I know somebody's stalking us," he grumbled.

Gaia's shoulders slumped. "Give me a break, Ed. Nobody's stalking—"

"Come *on*, you guys," Mary called impatiently.

Gaia opened her mouth to say something else, then closed it and turned to follow Mary.

Ed's lips turned downward. He shook his head. Hanging out with Mary all the time *was* having an effect on Gaia. She never would have acted this careless in the past. The old Gaia would have told everyone to go home. Then she would have sought out the bearded guy and kicked the crap out of him.

After that, they could have all enjoyed the rest of their winter break in peace.

But not the new Gaia. No. She opted for being a major pain in the ass. Before she met Mary, she used to listen to Ed. Now she didn't. Like when he'd told her about Charlie Salita. Had she paid any attention? No.

Now she was doing the same thing all over again. By not listening to Ed, she was walking right into another stupid situation. . . .

But apparently the new Gaia didn't learn from past mistakes.

The Freaks Come Out at Night

ALL OF CHINATOWN SMELLED LIKE ONE giant fried dumpling. Gaia's mouth couldn't stop watering. Every storefront window on the narrow street was packed with a brightly lit display of food: either a rack of hanging meats or ducklings or doughy pastries. Most of it looked fairly gross, of course, but the smell was incredible. She sucked in deep, huge breaths of the cold night air. She couldn't believe she'd never discovered this neighborhood. Chinatown was tailor-made for somebody like her—somebody who could pretty much live on desserts and fried foods until her heart gave out.

"I didn't know it was going to be so crowded," Mary said, raising her voice as she led Gaia and Ed through the throng of pedestrians on the sidewalk. She laughed once and glanced over her shoulder. "This is ridiculous. It's like Mardi Gras or something."

Gaia nodded, smiling. Coming here *was* like entering a foreign country. All the street and shop signs were in Chinese. The moment they turned off Mott Street onto Canal Street, every last trace of English vanished. And food was hardly the only exotic item being sold: There were all kinds of little trinkets and statues and electronic gadgets. . . .

"The freaks come out at night," Ed grumbled. "What are we even *doing* right now?"

Gaia didn't answer. Ed's sour mood was getting more irritating by the second. So he'd seen a guy with a beard in the park. Big deal. Even if the guy *had* been watching them, they were far from Greenwich Village right now. And it was hard to think of any place safer than a well-lit city street, packed with tourists.

"I'll tell you what we're doing," Mary stated, stopping in front of a butcher shop. The glass window featured a particularly nasty display of fatty sausage links hanging from the ceiling. "We're playing truth or dare." She turned around and shot Gaia a quick smile over Ed's head. "And Ed?" She nodded at the window. "I dare you to eat one of those sausages."

Gaia laughed. *That* would teach him not to complain.

"Don't I get to pick?" Ed protested. "I mean, it's truth *or* dare, right?"

Mary sighed disappointedly, folding her arms across her chest. "Fine, Ed. If you want to be totally boring . . ."

"If you ask me, those sausages look pretty good," Gaia joked.

Ed scowled up at her, but the faint beginnings of a smile appeared at the corners of his mouth. Finally, she thought. Maybe he was starting to lighten up a little. Maybe he could actually enjoy himself.

"Are you sure they're even meant for human beings?" he asked, rotating the wheelchair so that he faced the window directly. His eyes wandered up and down the display case. His face soured. "I mean—"

Without warning, he spun the wheelchair a full one hundred eighty degrees—so fast that the leg rest nearly grazed Gaia's shin.

"Jesus, Ed," she gasped, jumping back.

His eyes were wide. His face was a ghastly white.

"That guy!" he hissed.

Gaia exchanged a baffled glance with Mary. "What are you—"

"I j-just saw him," he sputtered. He tried to push himself higher up in the chair to get a better view. "In the window. I saw his reflection...."

"Are you *sure?*" Mary asked.

"Positive," Ed whispered. His voice was trembling. "He was right behind us—two seconds ago." He jerked a finger toward the intersection. "Walking that way."

Gaia stood on her tiptoes—scouring the mob with her eyes. But all she saw was the same swarming sea of tourists and Chinatown locals. "I don't know, Ed," she murmured. "Maybe—"

"I *saw* him, all right?" he yelled. "I'm positive. He's following us."

Gaia glanced back at Mary. "Did you see him?"

Mary shook her head, but she was a little pale, too. Gaia sighed. This was just great. Ed was making Mary paranoid, too—and Mary was edgy enough already. There were tons of scuzzy guys with long beards in New York, and most of them looked exactly alike: an army of bearded clones.

"I'm outta here," Ed announced. He spun his wheelchair onto the street with a quick, jerky motion. It rattled as it bounced off the curb.

"Come on, Ed." Gaia groaned. "If this guy's following us, how come he hasn't tried anything yet? I'm sure—"

"Maybe Ed's right," Mary interrupted quietly. "Maybe we should just go home." She wrapped her arms around herself. "It's pretty cold, anyway. And it's getting late."

Gaia sighed, waving her hands hopelessly. It wasn't that cold. Besides, it was never late in New York. Something was always happening. And Chinatown was a hot spot. For the first time since Gaia had moved to the city, she felt like she was a *part* of it— discovering it, unlocking all of its potential. More important, she wasn't focused entirely on herself and her own messed-up life. Sam Moon hadn't crossed her mind once. She didn't know when she'd get the opportunity to feel so Sam-free again. She wasn't about to let anyone blow it for her.

"What about the game?" she asked.

"The game is supposed to be *fun,* Gaia," Ed replied through tightly clenched teeth. "Even if I *am* imagining things, I'm not having fun. So there isn't much point in my playing, right?"

"That's true," Mary muttered, staring down at the ground.

"What are you *talking* about?" Gaia protested. "I'm having fun."

Ed sneered. "And everyone knows that Gaia Moore's fun takes precedence over all."

Gaia's eyes hardened. "What's *that* supposed to mean?"

"Nothing," he muttered. "Look, if you guys want to get shot or stabbed or raped, be my guests." He released the brakes on his wheelchair and struck out into the crowd. "I'm gone."

"Oh, come on," Gaia called after him. "I didn't mean …"

"Let him go," Mary said, grabbing Gaia's arm. "We shouldn't have invited him along, anyway. Let's just go back to my place, all right?"

Ed vanished into the night.

A queasy emptiness settled in Gaia's stomach. Maybe she had been a little harsh. She had thought she would never get into another serious fight with Ed Fargo—not after the whole Charlie Salita thing. And he'd been right about Charlie. But he was definitely wrong about this mysterious bearded stalker. No way would somebody follow Mary halfway across town without Gaia or Mary noticing. It was just too far-fetched. Besides, Ed was just overprotective. How many times had he proved that already?

BY THE TIME ED ROLLED THE MILE OR so up Broadway back to the West Village, his fury had subsided to a dull rage. His neck was starting to ache from shaking his head so much. He knew he must look like a lunatic, gesturing and

Speak of the Devil

muttering to himself, but he couldn't care less. His mind was in a haze.

He'd always known Gaia to be reckless. But never *stupid*. Even when she'd insisted on tracking down "the Gentleman"—that whacked-out serial killer who turned out to be the new kid in their class—she'd showed some kind of *logic*. Some kind of rational thinking.

All right, maybe not. It was hard to call vigilantism rational under any circumstances. But at least she'd been mildly concerned with her personal safety. Even when she'd agreed to go out with Charlie Salita and Sideburns Tim, she didn't believe she was making a bad choice. It had been stupid, yes, but not irrational.

Now she just didn't seem to give a shit about anything.

Whatever. It wasn't his problem. Nope. If she and Mary wanted to get killed at the hands of some fatso drug dealer, he'd just find a couple of other hot chicks to hang around with. This was a big city, right? His wheelchair bounced as he turned off Broadway onto Bond Street. Here were plenty of nice young women around. Normal women. Women who wouldn't endanger his life.

Maybe he could even meet some right now.

Sure. The Atomic Diner was just up the block on the right. He loved that place. It was one of those retro fifties joints, with minijukeboxes at each booth and an old-fashioned soda fountain. It was a favorite haunt among the hip Greenwich Village high school crowd.

He used to hang there a lot himself when he was going out with Heather. And he'd always secretly noted that she wasn't the only beautiful girl who liked to eat bacon and eggs at 10 P.M. on a Friday. . . .

He jerked to a stop. His eyes narrowed.

Speak of the devil.

Sitting right there, in the first window booth of the Atomic Diner, was none other than Heather herself.

She was stuffing her face with french fries and talking animatedly with somebody just out of view of the window frame. Probably Sam Moon. Ed bowed his head. Tonight was really his lucky night, wasn't it? First he got blown off by Gaia. Then he saw his ex-girlfriend whooping it up. Clearly Heather's being here was a sign. Yes. A sign that he should go straight home and lock himself away for the rest of the holiday season—

There was a loud rapping on the window.

Ed glanced up. *Oh, brother.* He should have moved more quickly. Heather had spotted him out there on the sidewalk, and now she was furiously waving at him, beckoning him to come in. He tried to force a smile. There were about a million things he'd rather do than hang out with Heather and Sam—including hard labor, prison time, calculus homework. . . . But it was no use: She'd trapped him. He nodded and sighed.

Wait a second. He did a double take as he scooted past the window.

Heather wasn't with Sam. She was with her older sister Phoebe. Ed's spirits immediately lifted. He hadn't seen Phoebe since the summer, when she'd come home for a break from college. He waved. She waved back. Whoa. She looked amazing. Didn't girls usually put on weight in college? If anything, Phoebe looked like she'd *dropped* fifteen pounds. She looked older, too, somehow—mature and exotic and skinny. Her long, brown hair hung far down her back, and she was wearing a wild-looking, floral blue dress.

He picked up his pace and rounded the corner, pushing through the diner door. The delicious odor of fried food wafted over him. Maybe this wouldn't be so bad after all. It was nice and warm in here . . . and besides, he'd always liked Phoebe. Yes. Phoebe was always very cool. She had an edge, and it was probably for that reason that she and Heather had never gotten along all that well, but deep down she was a lot more mellow and easygoing than her sister.

And way out of your league, bozo, he reminded himself, knowing full well where these thoughts were taking him. *Even before the accident. And she's a sophomore in college. Not to mention the fact that she's your ex-girlfriend's sister—and therefore necessarily in the "untouchable" category.*

"Hey, Ed!" Phoebe called as he rolled down the narrow aisle to their booth.

"Hey, Phoebe. What's up? You here for Christmas break?"

"Yeah." She smiled at him. "I see nothing's changed. You're still roaming the streets at night like a hoodlum."

"Looking for fights, no doubt," Heather chimed in brightly.

Ed smirked at Heather. "What are *you* so happy about?"

"Don't ask," Phoebe said, rolling her eyes. "She just came from her boyfriend's dorm."

"Oh." Ed cleared his throat. He felt a quick pang of two conflicting emotions—the same jealousy he always felt when he pictured Heather and Sam being together, but also a strange sort of relief. He'd thought that Sam and Heather were on the rocks. But if Sam was hanging out with Heather, that meant that he wouldn't be hanging out with Gaia. So Gaia would just have to find someone else to fall in love with.

Like me, for instance.

Ed shook his head. He was supposed to be *mad* at Gaia. Not obsessing over her.

"What's wrong?" Phoebe asked.

"Huh? Oh, nothing." He glanced at her dress, shoving Gaia from his thoughts. "What's up with the new threads? You aren't turning into a hippie on us, are you?"

She laughed. "As if. Why? You don't like it?" Ed was surprised by the question. Phoebe wasn't the type to care what people thought. She'd always been too confident for that. In fact, she'd always been a tad *over*confident.

"No, no, I like it a lot. It's just not your usual style."

"She's being brainwashed by her friends at SUNY, Ed," Heather remarked dryly, her mouth half full of fries. "I mean, look at what she's eating. She actually ordered a salad. I mean, who goes to a diner and orders a salad?"

"Good point." Ed leaned over and frowned at her plate. Not only had Phoebe ordered a salad; she'd barely touched it. Then again, he couldn't blame her. That heap of wilted green lettuce didn't look very appetizing. "Did you join some kind of vegetarian cult or something?"

"Very funny," Phoebe muttered. She grinned. "I just decided to go on a little diet. Besides, do you know how many years *one* order of Atomic Diner fries can take off your life?"

Ed laughed. "Is that the kind of thing they're teaching you in college?"

"That, and how to dress in clothes that went out of fashion before the first Woodstock," Heather replied. She shook her head in mock disdain.

"Hey, I like this dress," Phoebe said, giving her sister a playful kick under the table. "Besides, none of my old clothes fit me anymore."

"I like it, too," Heather grumbled with a smile. "I'm just jealous."

"Well, then, you'll just have to go to school in the fabulous metropolis of Binghamton, New York, too,"

Phoebe said. "I'll put you on a strict wheat germ diet and take you shopping for secondhand clothes, and we'll look like twins from a *Doublemint* commercial."

"Oh, goody!" Heather cried. "Just what I always wanted!"

Ed laughed again. It was amazing to see Heather and her sister actually getting along. And not only that—*he* was enjoying himself. He didn't think such a thing was possible. Especially tonight. Here he was, sitting with Heather and her sister, chatting and laughing. There wasn't any tension. None. For a few blissful, fleeting seconds he'd even managed to forget that he was in a wheelchair.

It was a good thing he'd ditched Gaia after all.

Well . . . no, it wasn't. But at least he could pretend it was for the next few minutes.

SKIZZ.

There was no doubt in Mary's mind: Ed had seen Skizz. The pig hadn't been kidding about coming to find her. He'd probably been following her all day. For all Mary knew, he could be lurking outside the apartment building right now.

High Security

She stood at her bedroom window, staring down at the lights of Park Avenue. She didn't see any people out there—but Skizz was clever. The twenty-four hours he'd given her to pay him back had long since expired. At least this was a high-security building. Her door was dead bolted. Besides, there was a doorman. There were video cameras. All the doorman had to do was press a button, and the police would rush right over. . . .

". . . should call him," Gaia was saying.

"Huh?" Mary tore her attention from the street below and glanced back at Gaia's sprawled form on the unmade bed. "Sorry. What was that?"

"Maybe I should call Ed," Gaia murmured, staring up at Mary's ceiling. "I feel bad. I guess I just kind of got caught up in the game."

Mary walked over and sat on the edge of the mattress. "You know, Gaia, we don't have to keep playing." She bit her lip, debating whether or not to tell Gaia about Skizz's call. No. It was best not to think about it. Besides, there was a chance that his threats were empty. And even if they weren't, this was *her* problem. Not Gaia's. She didn't want to drag Gaia into the middle of it—especially after Skizz's warning about the "psycho blond chick."

"But I *want* to keep playing," Gaia stated.

"But maybe for Ed's sake . . ." Mary let the sentence hang.

"You don't believe him, do you?" Gaia asked. She sat up straight, her eyes narrowing. "Did you see something, too?"

"No." Mary sighed and shook her head.

"Then what are you worried about?"

"It's just . . ." Mary lowered her eyes. It felt terrible to keep her feelings bottled up inside her. She could at least let Gaia in on her thoughts without going into all the gory details. And as a friend, Gaia had a right to know why she was acting so strange. "Remember that guy you beat up the night we met?"

Gaia nodded. "How could I forget?" she murmured.

"Well, I owe him money . . . ," she said.

"Is that it?" Gaia asked.

Mary frowned. "Well, yeah, but—"

"Don't worry," Gaia said soothingly. "He won't try anything. That guy is *useless*. In case you've forgotten, I kicked his ass in the span of about five seconds."

Mary didn't look convinced.

"Besides," Gaia added, "I'm sure he's heard that you're clean now. So you're of no use to him, you know?"

"Maybe," Mary said dubiously. "But Skizz doesn't forget about things like money."

Gaia was silent for a moment. "How much do you owe him?" she finally asked.

"Five hundred," Mary whispered.

"I bet that's a drop in the bucket to guys like that,"

Gaia reassured her. "Trust me. And if you're thinking about all this because of Ed . . . don't. He's the most paranoid guy on the planet."

Mary tried to force a smile. But the sad fact of the matter was that her friend had no idea what she was talking about. And Gaia had the benefit of thinking she was invincible—a trait Mary didn't share. She would be safe inside her room or with Gaia around to protect her—but someday, at some moment, she'd find herself alone on the streets.

That was when Skizz would strike. She was sure of it.

RED SQUARE WAS PACKED WITH PEOPLE,

Anonymous Tip

but Tom Moore knew that this was to be expected. He welcomed the crowds. Witnesses would ensure the safety of this meeting. Not that he was worried about security, but he knew that his contact had some concerns. Debra (at least that was her alias) was still new to this theater of operations, new to the job itself. And young. In fact, she reminded him a little of Katia. Beautiful and innocent. Naive . . .

He thrust the thoughts aside. He would not think of Katia. Not now. He would concentrate on the task at hand.

As he hurried across the cobblestones in the direction of the multicolored spires of St. Basil's cathedral, he was surprised by how many American voices he heard. Of course, the week after Christmas marked the height of the tourist season—in spite of the frigid temperatures. And since Russia was no longer a closed and communist society, tourism was one of the few industries that kept its economy afloat.

Tourism and terrorism, of course.

He raised his eyes in the biting wind, glancing up at the cathedral. Even after having seen it so many times, he was still struck by its fairy-tale beauty: the brilliant reds and greens and golds, all of the different turrets and ornate fixtures. . . . It looked less like a place of worship and more like an enchanted castle. He snaked his way through a mob of students toward the southeast entrance: the rendezvous point. But then he paused.

Debra wasn't there.

Protocol dictated that she should be the first to arrive. For a moment he stood still and sized up his surroundings. As far as he could tell, he wasn't being watched or followed. There was no need to panic . . . not yet. There was a chance that she could have been held up in traffic. Public transportation in Moscow was notoriously unreliable.

He stepped closer to the cathedral's massive arched doorway. The biting wind stung his ears, but he hardly noticed. A few people jostled him. Where *was* she? The entire operation hinged on this one exchange. She *knew* that. The agency was counting on her. She had managed to acquire a copy of the smugglers' safety deposit box key. The box contained the money they would exchange for the plutonium.

But Debra didn't know the location of the bank. Only Tom knew that. Each member of the unit was entrusted with one vital piece of information; that way the entire operation wouldn't be compromised if one of them were caught. Still . . . if she failed to deliver the key in time, then Tom would be unable to prevent the smugglers from leaving the country. And they were leaving soon. This afternoon, in fact. They would have all the cash they needed to buy anything they wanted—

A muffled beep rang from deep inside his coat pocket. He scowled. That was probably Debra, calling to explain why she was late. He fished out his cell phone and flipped it open.

"Yes?" he muttered.

"Hello, Tom."

He stiffened. It wasn't Debra. It was a man. And whoever he was, he wasn't part of the agency. The agency never addressed its operatives by name over the phone.

"Tom?" the man asked. "Are you there?"

"Yes," Tom croaked, feeling a sudden dreaded certainty that Debra would never arrive, that she had been killed. The voice was American . . . but Tom couldn't place it. From the static, he judged the call was coming from overseas.

" I'm listening."

"It's about Gaia."

Jesus Christ. It took all of Tom's years of training, all of his carefully honed self-control, not to display any emotion. But he could no longer breathe. He gripped the phone as tightly as he could. He felt like his heart had been set ablaze.

"Go on," Tom choked out. He barely recognized his own voice.

"Your brother's moving against her," the man said.

Tom drew in a deep, quivering breath. Loki. He should have known. He was clever. Obviously he was well aware that Tom was halfway around the world, unable to stop him.

"He's placed someone very close to her," the voice went on. "An operative whom Gaia would never suspect."

"Who?" Tom hissed. "I don't have time—"

The line went dead.

"Hello?" Tom barked. "Hello?"

He stared at the cathedral door. Still no sign of Debra. It could mean only one thing. She was dead.

She had to be. Tom dialed the agency's emergency number as quickly as he could.

"Go," a voice answered.

"Three, zulu, alpha, four, seven," Tom whispered—the code for a failed operation. It was surprisingly easy.

"Understood," the voice replied.

Tom folded the cell phone and jammed it back in his pocket. Suddenly nothing mattered anymore—nothing but Loki and Gaia. The rest of the world ceased to exist.

Without so much as a backward glance, he turned and hurried from Red Square.

Hang on, Gaia, he silently implored. *I'll be there soon.*

I used to think that I was lucky
in a way because I had already
experienced the worst possible
thing that could ever happen to
me. Some people coast through
life—then when they're forty or
something, they're suddenly hit
with a disfiguring disease or a
heart attack or they lose all
their money. And since their
lives have basically been gravy
up to that point, they're totally
unequipped to deal with it. They
have a complete mental breakdown.
It's institution time.
Electroshock therapy.
Straitjackets. The works.

   Not me, though. I figured
since I already suffered one of
the most major catastrophes known
to man, the rest of my life would
be pretty good by comparison.
Nothing could make me feel any
lower than losing the use of my
legs. Especially since my entire
life was pretty much devoted to
skateboarding. To quote the old
cliché: When you've hit rock bottom,

there's no place to go but up. I guess it helped me deal with the last two years. Thinking that way kept *me* out of an institution.

Now I know that I was wrong.

No matter how much pain you endure, something else can come along to knock you back down. Something totally different and unexpected. It doesn't even have to be physical pain. It can be something as simple as getting into a fight with somebody.

But there's no point in dwelling on the negatives. You'll just drive yourself crazy.

Well, not
tonight.
Her heart
pounded.
Oh, no.
It was
time to
make
Daddy
proud
again.

**over
the
edge**

Fear

GAIA COULD SEE THE FEAR CLEARLY ETCHED on Mary's face. It was right there: right in her creased forehead and downcast eyes. They had been speeding downtown on the local number-six train for nearly fifteen minutes, and Mary hadn't spoken once. She was more worried about this drug dealer than she'd admitted. Probably thanks to Ed.

Gaia knew all about fear. She'd seen it enough on people's faces to know the signs. And she'd also studied it. Scientifically. She'd read that the best way to overcome it was to confront it directly, head-on . . . to embrace it.

It was a lesson from the *Go Rin No Sho*—the "Book of Five Rings"—a Japanese guide to martial arts. Her father used to make her read it all the time. Most of the books were about as thrilling as the yellow pages and about as heavy, too—like *Leviathan* and *The Iliad*. Her dad was a stickler for the classics. But the *Go Rin No Sho* was different. Gaia had loved it from the time she was a little girl. It was beautifully written, like poetry. It taught that a person would never be complete unless they explored both good and evil. Darkness and light.

It made perfect sense. To her, at least.

Maybe that was why she remembered the lesson about fear so well. Since she didn't feel fear, she could never confront it. But she realized something: Even if *she* was unable to use fear as a tool, she could help Mary use it.

"So we're still playing, right?" Gaia asked over the rattle of the speeding train wheels.

"Huh?" Mary asked.

Gaia shifted in her seat, trying to get comfortable. It was impossible. Even though she generally loved the subways, rush hour was always a nightmare. Somehow she found herself mushed between Mary and some businessman's designer leather briefcase. The sharp corner was starting to dig into her sides. But they were almost at Astor Place—the stop closest to Washington Square Park. She could endure a few more minutes of torture.

"The game?" Gaia prompted.

"Oh—yeah, yeah. Of course." Mary nodded as she stared down at the forest of legs rising from the grimy subway floor. "But do you think we can avoid the park? Just for tonight? We can go back tomorrow."

"And why would we avoid the park?" Gaia asked gently.

"Because I'm scared of running into Skizz," Mary admitted.

"I think that's exactly why we *should* go to the park," Gaia countered. "Look, chances are he won't even be there. And even if he is, he won't try anything. And even if he *does,* I'll kick his ass, all right?"

Mary smirked. "I guess I don't have a choice, do I?"

"No," Gaia replied dryly. The train began to slow. She glanced out the window. The lights of the Astor Street station swam into view. The wheels squeaked harshly. "So here's what. I dare you to go back to the spot where we first met—and sing a song of your choice by Hanson at the top of your lungs."

For a moment Mary looked at her as if she were completely insane. Gaia couldn't blame her. She didn't even know where that dare had come from. It had just sort of popped out of her head.

"Hanson?" Mary started laughing. "But that's not fair. I don't even *know* any songs by Han—"

"Then make one up," Gaia interrupted. "Or sing a song by Michael Jackson. Any ridiculous song will do." She grabbed Mary's arm and pulled her up along with her, then began snaking her way through the crowded car.

"What if I want to pick truth?" Mary asked.

Gaia looked her straight in the eye as the doors slid open. "You don't really want to pick truth, do you? I mean, this is a chance to sing in public, right?"

"I don't know, Gaia. . . ."

"Look, by daring you to do something silly in the same spot where you last saw Skizz, you'll see that you have nothing to worry about. And once you see that you're safe, you'll realize that you can start getting on with your life."

WHAT THE HELL AM I THINKING? MARY
wondered.

Here she was, about to sing **Lightbulb**
a song (she didn't even know
what song)—and there was a
very good chance that by calling attention to herself,
she would send Skizz running straight for her, like a
moth to a lightbulb.

She walked silently with Gaia down Eighth Street,
with her head down to protect her face from the bitter wind. The air was so cold that it felt antiseptic,
bluish. The night was eerily quiet. Her eyes smarted.
Her nose burned. She kept her gaze pinned to the
sidewalk. She couldn't believe she had actually let
Gaia talk her into this. If Skizz was anywhere in the
city, he'd be *here*.

But at the same time, in spite of her anxiety, she
couldn't help but feel a peculiar anticipation. And
somewhere in the dim recesses of her consciousness,
she knew that the anxiety and anticipation were all
bound up together in the same feeling. It was a feeling
all her own—a *selfish* feeling, one that was bent
on seeking pleasure, no matter what the
risk. It was the same one she used to get when she
diced out a line of coke. Or met Skizz on some dark
corner to make a score . . .

It was the one she got knowing that she was
putting herself in harm's way.

And that was the root of her problem. Of all her problems, really. Very simply put, the closer she was to danger, the more she felt alive. That was bad. Very bad. She had to suppress that feeling. She shook her head as they turned south onto Fifth Avenue. Once she started slipping down that slope, there was no telling *what* she could do.

"Piece of cake," Gaia murmured, patting her shoulder.

"Yeah," Mary whispered. "Right." She glanced up. The Arc de Triomphe loomed ahead of her at the end of the block, brightly lit against the purplish, starless sky. Behind the white marble the park was a shadowy black abyss. She swallowed.

"All you gotta do is go in there and sing," Gaia said with a perfectly straight face. "I mean really open up. Let the entire West Village hear your dulcet tones."

Mary had to laugh. But she found she was trembling. Of course, that was the weather's fault. The chill tonight soaked through her coat, down past her skin, all the way to the center of her bones. She paused on the corner opposite the park entrance.

"And why, exactly, am I doing this again?" she asked. Her question billowed from her mouth in a frozen white cloud, then vanished under the streetlamps.

Gaia raised her eyebrows. "Because I dared you to," she said with a smile.

GAIA KNEW THAT MARY WAS AFRAID.

But as she watched Mary trudge into the park alone, she knew that the more fear she felt, the better it would be in the long run. The greater the risk, the greater the reward.

Besides, Mary was in no real danger. First of all, the park was completely deserted. Only a lunatic would be hanging out there on a night like tonight—a night so cold that the tips of your fingers and toes went numb after about three minutes. Also, as Gaia had told Mary, if some creep *did* try anything, she would be right there. Ready to knock him flat. From where she was waiting on MacDougal Street, she could see the entire park—and Mary would never be out of her sight, not even for an instant.

She smiled as Mary sat on a park bench in a circular pool of pale light. Good. By singing a ridiculous song and freezing her butt off in that exact spot, she would drive out her fear of Skizz. It was like a ritual, an exorcism. And Mary Moss would emerge from it a new woman.

THIS WASN'T THE EXACT SPOT WHERE MARY had last seen Skizz face-to-face, but she figured it was close enough. Gaia wasn't that nitpicky. **Close**

She hunched over and squeezed herself, struggling to fight the cold. Her teeth chattered uncontrollably. So. She had to rack her brain for a song. The problem was, she didn't *listen* to Hanson. But she had to sing something—otherwise Gaia would never let her out of the park. For some reason, though, she couldn't seem of think of anything. Her mind was a complete blank.

Mary had never been the creative type. She always hated this kind of thing, being forced to perform on the spot. That was probably another reason she'd loved coke so much, now that she thought about it. Up. One little bump, and your thoughts moved at the speed of light. For those five minutes you were a genius. Not only a genius; a world-class singer, too. No song, no matter how out of tune and excruciating, was ever *that* bad when you were wired. Of course not. It was brilliant. . . .

She shivered, frowning. As usual, thinking about cocaine was getting her nowhere. The sooner she started singing, the sooner she could get the hell out of this frozen wasteland.

"If you wanna be my lover," she sang quietly. She knew it was lame, but she couldn't help herself. It would have to do. *"You gotta get with my friends—"*

Suddenly she felt a presence behind her.

"Gaia?"

She looked behind her—nothing. Mary glanced toward where Gaia stood at the edge of the park. Her friend was there, hugging herself and shivering but also grinning from ear to ear.

At least one of them wasn't completely paranoid, Mary thought. She turned back toward the empty park.

"Uh, *friendship lasts forever . . .*"

A finger tapped her on the shoulder. Mary smiled. Gaia had finally realized this was cruel and unusual punishment.

She took a bow toward the empty square, but as she stood up to turn, she noticed she could still see Gaia way over at the edge of the park, fiddling with her coat buttons.

Mary opened her mouth to scream Gaia's name, but it only came out in a whisper.

GAIA DIDN'T SEE THE SHADOWY MALE form creeping up on Mary until it was right behind her. She was concentrating too hard to hear whatever the hell it was that Mary was singing. Jesus. Where had he come from? She was *trained* to spot people in the night.

She sucked in her breath and bolted across the street, hurtling the low park fence in one fluid motion. Whoever he was, he must have been hiding. Waiting. And whoever he was, he was large. Fat, almost. And familiar . . .

136

Shit. There it was. The beard. Even with his back to her, she could see a tangle of greasy hairs flapping in the wind. She broke into a sprint.

It was him.

"I . . . I . . . ," MARY SPUTTERED IN HORROR.

Panic

She couldn't move. Her teeth stopped chattering; her body stopped trembling. Her limbs were too tense, frozen solid. For all her fear and worry, she just hadn't truly believed Skizz would be here. It was just too *obvious*, somehow—too predictable. Like walking into a trap. A trap laid expressly for her. Life wasn't that simple.

"Who's Gay-uh?"

Mary could only shake her head. Skizz looked even more foul than she'd remembered. His skin was blotchy, covered with scabs. His beady eyes bore down on her from within the fat folds of his face. And the wispy ends of his beard spread in every direction. Instinctively her eyes flashed to his hands. Both were jammed into the pockets of his down jacket. *Oh God.* Something besides his hand was also stuffed in the right pocket. Something pointy.

"I'm asking you a question," he growled.

"Sh-She . . . she's nobody," Mary stuttered, unable to tear her eyes from the pocket.

"Look at me," he barked.

She flinched. Her eyes darted to his face.

All at once he smiled—revealing an uneven row of yellow teeth. "I'm sorry, baby," he murmured. "I'm being rude. It's none of my business. So let's just take care of *our* business, and I'll be on my way. Then you can go back to your little birthday celebration."

Mary opened her mouth, but panic had robbed her of speech.

Skizz looked up for a moment, glancing furtively in either direction down the darkened path. He withdrew his right hand from the coat. Clutched in his chubby fingers was a small, shiny pistol—no bigger than a toy, a water gun. It glittered in the cold light of the park lamps.

A last gasp of air escaped Mary's lungs. She couldn't breathe anymore.

"Now, I'm assuming you came here to pay me back," he whispered. He laughed humorlessly. "There ain't no other reason a rich girl like you would come out in this cold. Gotta be drugs or money. So let's see the cash. *All* of it."

But I don't have it, she answered silently. *I swear—*

He cocked the pistol. "Now."

Rage

THE INSTANT GAIA SAW THE GLINT OF
metal, her pace doubled. She was barely
conscious of the ground flying under her
feet. Her mind was totally focused on the
figure of the drug dealer, hunched over the
back of the bench where Mary sat.

Time slowed to a crawl.

Gaia was sick with rage. It was *her* fault that Mary
was in danger. *Her* fault that Mary might get killed.
She had pushed Mary into this situation—back into
the world Mary had left behind, and now she might
die because of it. Never before had Gaia felt such
anger. And all of it was directed at herself. If he pulled that trigger . . .

But no. She wouldn't allow it. She was almost upon
him. Her muscles tensed. She knew exactly how she
was going to strike: a flying sidekick to the back that
would send him flipping over the bench.

Her legs pumped to a fever pitch—then lifted from
the ground, slowly and gracefully, like the retraction of
a plane's landing gear after takeoff. For a wondrous instant she was airborne. She thrust out her right leg,
straightening so that the side of her foot would con-
nect. . . .

Now.

"AAAH!"

Mary heard Skizz's bloodcurdling scream at the exact same moment she realized he was no longer standing behind her; he was flying *over* her.

Rescue

She threw her hands over her head and cringed, watching in terror as he tumbled through the air and landed flat on his back. The gun clattered away from him into the shadows.

And then she saw Gaia—gracefully somersaulting across the pavement.

Warmth surged through Mary's body. She should have known Gaia would come to her rescue. Gaia would teach Skizz about trying to collect on a debt from a recovering addict. It was ass-kicking time. And not a moment too soon.

GAIA CROUCHED OVER THE DRUG DEALER'S body in the most basic kung fu stance— legs bent, arms up, right hand poised above the left. Her breathing was slow and even. The electric fizz tingled in her veins

Trick

the way it always did before combat, but there was something different tonight.

She was oddly calm.

Her rage hadn't subsided. Yet it gave her an edge. Almost as if she were watching the events unfold from a distance . . . watching as this `fat, middle-aged piece of shit` staggered to his feet. How could she have been so stupid? She'd forgotten the rules of combat she'd had pounded into her head since she could remember. *Always* be ready. *Always* be alert. Instead she'd been reckless and self-indulgent, using her skills for petty pranks and leading her friend into a deadly trap.

All those years of her father's painstaking training were going to waste.

All those afternoons spent in their backyard—repeating kick after kick, block after block. . . . She was supposed to be disciplined. A *machine*. She'd allowed her dear father's education to slip away. `She'd lost the very thing that had turned her into a monster.` Yes. There was no denying it. She'd become sloppy in her teenage years.

Well, not tonight. Her heart pounded. Oh, no. It was time to make Daddy proud again.

She smiled at the drug dealer.

He straightened, wincing—clutching his back. Suddenly he froze. His eyes narrowed. "*You*," he spat. "You're that bitch."

"That's right," Gaia murmured. "I'm that bitch."

He lunged forward, swinging with his right hand.

Gaia almost laughed. He'd telegraphed that punch

so blatantly that she didn't even need to block it. She simply ducked out of the way, sidestepping him. The force of his own effort sent him staggering across the pavement.

He whirled around. His eyes smoldered.

He was breathing heavily, filling the air with white vapor. "You just better pray you don't get hurt," he hissed. "You don't know who you're messin' with."

I think I do, Gaia thought. But she kept silent. Talking during a fight was a distraction. Besides, silence instilled fear in an opponent. Not that she needed any advantages over him. He was scared enough. With good reason. He had no idea what was coming.

"Careful, Gaia," Mary murmured from the bench. "There's a gun on the ground."

The drug dealer grinned.

Oh, please. Did he really think Gaia was that stupid? Obviously he didn't know where the gun was. Otherwise he'd be looking at it.

Again he jumped forward and threw his right fist at her face.

How original, Gaia thought. There was no need to block *this* punch, either—but she wasn't interested in toying with him any longer. She shifted to the left and grabbed his wrist in midair, simultaneously kicking his right shin. It was classic kung fu. One of her patent moves. The force of his own punch in combination with the kick sent him flying off balance. But she didn't let go of his hand. Instead she twisted it, holding him in place—supporting almost all his weight. She grunted. Damn, he was heavy.

They were face-to-face.

Gaia grimaced. She could smell his rancid breath. Still, she savored the moment. By now he'd guessed that he couldn't possibly defeat her.

She let go of him. He nearly fell.

In the split second that he fought to regain his balance, she decided to switch from kung fu to karate. With an almost clinical detachment she chose to end this boring fight with a technique straight out of the *Go Rin No Sho*. A trick.

She raised her right fist.

He stared at it, backing off slightly.

She struck with her left.

The hand whistled audibly as it sliced through the frozen air toward his neck.

Contact. All of her years of training went into that strike—straight to the pressure point. She felt his collarbone shatter, heard the soft cracking sounds. It felt like gravel under the soft layer of his blubbery flesh.

"Uhh!" he gurgled.

He sank to his knees. His eyes were wide in shock. His mouth fell open. He gaped up at her, shaking his head. But she felt no pity. He deserved this—for torturing Mary when she was trying to get clean, for hooking others on drugs, for making the world a sadder and more desperate place. They *all* deserved this . . . everyone who caused suffering, everyone who profited from other people's misery.

"Gaia?"

Mary's voice drifted out of the night. But it was as if Gaia heard it in a dream. Time slowed again; there was no future, no past—only a continuous present in which she needed to finish her opponent. That, too, was a lesson from the *Go Rin No Sho*. She could recite the lines word for word. She could almost see the page in front of her as she drew back her left leg: "*Strike with the left side, with the spirit resolved, until the enemy is dead. . . .*"

The drug dealer lifted one hand, using the other one to clutch his ruined shoulder. "No," he wheezed. His lungs labored heavily. "Please, stop—"

Her leg lashed out in a powerful kick. The tip of her toe connected just under his chin. Blood splattered from his mouth. But amazingly enough, he didn't cry out. He made absolutely no sound. His body hung in midair, with his head thrown back, eyes staring at the sky—then he collapsed backward, hitting the pavement with a sticky smack.

"*Gaia!*" Mary shrieked.

Gaia stared down at him. The drug dealer's eyes were closed now. He lay perfectly still.

"What are you doing?" Mary's voice rose. "Stop it! Stop it!"

Gaia turned to answer her friend—but at that moment the ground beneath her seemed to open up and swallow her whole.

TWO DEAD BODIES. TWO.

That's what I'm dealing with.

Nightmare

Mary sat on the bench, still unable to move. Her eyes flashed from one crumpled form to the other. Time to rewind. She couldn't understand what had just happened. Gaia suddenly went into psycho kung fu mode, and then ... *what?* Both she and Skizz looked like ghosts. They were bone white. Skizz's blood glistened in black puddles on the pavement. His mouth was open. Several teeth were missing. Neither he nor Gaia seemed to be breathing. Mary knew *she* was breathing because her breath was quite visible—exploding from her nostrils in a rapid, doglike rhythm. She was practically hyperventilating—

There!

A faint, grayish puff drifted from Skizz's unmoving lips.

Mary held her breath.

A few seconds later there was another puff. Then another. Skizz groaned.

Okay. Mary swallowed. *He isn't dead. This is good. Very good. Fatally injured, maybe—but not dead. Not yet, anyway. That left Gaia. . . .*

Mary jumped up and crouched beside her. She couldn't panic. No. The last time Gaia had beat up Skizz, she had also keeled over—for no apparent reason. Mary had thought that Gaia was on coke, actually. At the time it seemed like the only reasonable explanation for her inexplicable behavior.

Of course, that beating had been a slap on the wrist compared to this.

But maybe Gaia's passing out was some kind of physical problem. Like an allergic reaction or something. Yeah. The harder Gaia pounded on somebody, the worse she suffered. And now Mary remembered that Gaia had avoided the subject of that first collapse—

"Oh, man," Gaia mumbled.

"Yes!" Mary whispered. Hot tears welled in her eyes. She reached out and grabbed Gaia's hand. *My God.* The skin was so cold. . . .

Gaia opened an eyelid. "Are you okay?" she croaked.

"Me?" Mary hissed, glancing around. The question was almost funny, it was so absurd. But the situation was far from humorous. The park was still deserted. Her eyes fell on Skizz. He wasn't moving. He was still breathing, though. Barely.

"Yeah," Gaia answered. "He didn't do anything—"

146

"We gotta get out of here," Mary hissed urgently. "I think you hurt Skizz really bad."

Gaia clutched at Mary's arm and tried to pull herself into an upright position. She coughed a few times. She blinked at Skizz.

"Oh, no," she murmured shakily. Her entire body quivered. Mary couldn't help but notice that her neck was dotted with goose bumps. "I didn't mean . . ."

Mary shook her head. "It—it doesn't matter," she stammered. She could feel her pulse rising, feel her face getting hot—even though the temperature must have been close to zero. Gaia looked so disturbed, so unsure of herself. What the hell had happened, anyway? What had pushed her so far over the edge? The entire evening was starting to feel less like reality and more like some horrible nightmare. Mary fought to stay in control. "We gotta get out of here, Gaia. I mean it. This is really bad. . . ."

Gaia slumped against her. "You're gonna have to help me," she gasped.

"All right." Summoning all of her strength, Mary grabbed Gaia by the waist and hauled her to her feet. "Do you think you can walk?"

"I'll . . . try." Gaia flung an arm around Mary's shoulders. She felt like a giant rag doll in Mary's grip—floppy and out of control. But Mary squeezed her as tightly as she could.

"All we have to do is get to your house, okay?"

Mary pleaded urgently. "It's not far at all. We can figure this all out when we get there."

Gaia nodded. "We gotta call 911. He's in really bad shape. . . ."

"We will. We will." Mary shambled down the path toward the south exit, struggling to drag Gaia beside her. The girl could barely move. She was like a zombie. Catatonic.

The two of them nearly stepped on Skizz's face.

"I'm so sorry, Mary," Gaia whispered. "I'm so sorry—"

"It's all right," Mary interrupted.

But she was lying. It wasn't all right. Nothing was all right.

Until now, I never understood the worst part about being
fearless.

It's that I'm not afraid of
myself. And I should be. I should
be terrified of myself.
Especially after what I did to
that drug dealer in the park.

I just pray he lives. No, *pray*
is the wrong word. I don't believe in prayer. I don't believe
you can petition a higher power
(if there even is a higher power,
which I doubt) by clasping your
hands together and getting on
your knees.

But I hope the guy lives. I
really do.

And I wish I could tell Mary
what happened out there, why I
did what I did, but the truth is
that I have no idea. That ought
to scare me, too.

It doesn't, though. How can it?

Loki smiled again. Every operative knew what it meant to be **problem** removed from an **solved** assignment. It meant removal from existence.

Partial Confessional

"I DON'T SEE ANYTHING ABOUT IT IN THE paper," Mary mumbled. "So maybe he's okay."

Gaia sat slumped at the Nivenses' little kitchen table, staring across a soggy bowl of Froot Loops as Mary feverishly scoured the newspaper for any word of `Skizz's death`. Harsh winter sunlight streamed through the windows. Gaia didn't feel like mentioning that *The New York Times* probably wouldn't bother to report the death of a drug dealer. She didn't want to upset Mary any more than necessary. But the truth of the matter was that drug dealers got beat up and killed all the time in New York. It was a hazard of the business.

Still, if Mary believed that Skizz was okay, then she might calm down. And if Mary was calm, then maybe Gaia could convince herself that Skizz was okay, too.

Yeah. Sure.

I might have killed a man.

She'd been up all night, repeating those same words to herself over and over again, like some kind of `twisted mantra`. She hadn't slept. The fight had left her utterly spent—but she couldn't stop thinking about that look on his face after she'd kicked him. . . .

But he'd been breathing. Yes. She definitely

remembered seeing his feeble gasps in the night air. So there was a chance he could have lived. Hopefully their call to 911 hadn't been too late.

"The problem is, I don't know his real name," Mary murmured distractedly, flipping through the Metro section to the obituaries. She held the paper up in front of her face. "I think it was James something. . . ."

Gaia's bleary eyes fell to the brightly colored mush in her cereal bowl. Blech. For once she had absolutely no appetite. George had left a carton of minidoughnuts out on the counter as well—but even *those* didn't look tempting. She sighed and grabbed her bowl, then dumped its contents into the garbage and tossed it in the kitchen sink.

Mary flinched at the clatter.

"Sorry," Gaia mumbled.

"It's okay." Mary folded the paper and laid it in front of her. Her hair was stringy, disheveled. Her face was still as pale as it was the night before. Her freckles seemed to stand out in relief on her white skin. Dark circles ringed her eyes. Jesus. She looked as bad as Gaia felt. "Hey, are George and Ella going to be coming back anytime soon?"

Gaia shrugged. "Who knows?" She sighed and sat back down. The important thing was that they were gone. There was no *way* she could deal with either of them right now. George would probably try to have some misguided heart-to-heart, and Ella would probably bawl her out for wasting a serving of breakfast cereal. But there was no point in getting angry over imaginary events. She had plenty to worry about in real life. She nodded at the paper. "You know, I don't think you're gonna find his name in there even if he *did* die," she muttered.

"I know," Mary whispered. "I was just . . ." She didn't finish.

"Maybe we should go look for him," Gaia suggested.

Mary nodded grimly. "Yeah. I was thinking about that."

Gaia ran a hand through the tangled blond mess on her head. "The problem is . . ."

"If we find him, and he *is* okay . . ."

Their gazes met across the table. There was no need to complete the thought. If Skizz had indeed survived that attack—and if he was out of the hospital and out on the streets—well, then, he would have only one mission in life. Revenge.

"Gaia?" Mary's voice was soft, shaky. She leaned across the table. "Look, I know you hate talking about yourself and revealing your deep, dark secrets or whatever, but . . . but the thing is . . . I mean, what made you freak out like that?"

Gaia stared back at her. She blinked a few times. She'd known Mary was going to ask that question sooner or later. It was actually pretty amazing that Mary had waited so long. And she deserved to know. Even though Gaia hated confessionals more than she hated hanging out with Ella, she figured she owed Mary *some* kind of explanation.

At the very least she had to soothe Mary's fears that such an attack would never happen again. And if she tried to articulate what she did, then maybe she would understand her own actions better herself.

"I really don't know," Gaia whispered, staring down at the newspaper. "It was just a lot of things, really." She drew in a deep breath and raised her eyes. "But mostly . . . mostly it was that I felt responsible for putting you in danger. I was mad at myself. I just took it out on him."

Mary shook her head. "But it wasn't your fault. I mean, I didn't *have* to go into that park. I could have said no—"

"But I pushed you," Gaia insisted. She tried to smile. "And the thing was, I thought I was actually doing you a favor. I know that sounds crazy, but it's true. I thought that if you went into the park and nothing happened, you wouldn't be scared of Skizz anymore." Any trace of her smile vanished. "And look what happened."

"You saved my life, though," Mary pointed out. She swallowed, drumming her fingers on the wooden tabletop. "I mean, even in the worst-case scenario, you know, even if he doesn't make it . . . you *were* protecting me. He had a gun. It was self-defense."

"Right," Gaia whispered emptily. "Self-defense." Guilt chewed through her like some kind of flesh-eating disease. Mary's words were a lie. Gaia didn't have to defend herself; she could have scared that guy off with one punch.

"It *was*," Mary stated. But she might just have been trying to reassure herself. She slouched back in her chair and eyed Gaia curiously. "You know, you never told me. Where did you learn to fight like that, anyway?"

"My father," Gaia grumbled.

"Really?" All at once Mary sat up straight. Her gaze took on a new intensity. "The way you talk about him, it sounds like he knew everything about everything."

Gaia couldn't help but laugh. "Yeah. Sort of." She didn't try to mask the bitterness in her voice. "He instructed me in a lot of things."

"Like what?"

"Like . . ." Gaia hesitated. Amazingly enough, discussing her father wasn't nearly as painful as she would have imagined. It actually felt *good* to talk about him. And it wasn't as if Mary was trying to get information from Gaia for any sinister purposes; she simply wanted to know as much as possible about her friend. It was perfectly natural. Especially since Gaia hardly ever talked.

"Well, he made me read a lot," Gaia continued. She lifted her shoulders. "He basically made me do things that most kids shouldn't have to do until they're a lot older. Or not at all."

"Why?" Mary persisted.

Gaia laughed again. "Beats the hell out of me. I'd like to ask him myself."

"Why can't you?"

"Because I haven't seen the son of a bitch in five years."

The words flew from Gaia's mouth even before she was aware of saying them. *Damn.* She blinked. She hadn't realized the depths of her own venom. She was surprised. But most of all, she was surprised she had revealed so much. Had she made a mistake? Mary didn't need to know all the specifics. And Gaia certainly didn't need to discuss them. It had been a reflex; she couldn't help it—

"What happened?" Mary whispered.

Gaia's eyes fell back to the newspaper. A bitter bile rose in her throat. A stream of disjointed images floated through her consciousness: her mother's flowing dark hair . . . the delighted sound of her father's voice at the chess table in their cozy little wood-frame house: *"Katia! Our little girl is going to grow up to be a grand master!"* . . . a roaring fireplace . . . a terrible, driving snow that obliterated everything—

"No."

Mary blinked. "What?"

Gaia stared up at her. Had she said "no" out loud? She must have. This was not good. Thinking about her father would inevitably lead to her thinking about her mother, about that final night—and she was in no condition to go down that road. Not now. Not ever.

"I'm sorry," Mary murmured. "I don't mean to pry."

Gaia shook her head. "No . . . no, it's just that . . .

my—my father's a lousy guy," she stammered. Her throat tightened. "End of story."

Mary nodded. "I understand."

No, you don't, Gaia thought. Her mind was in a very dark cloud. *And you never should have to understand about people like him—people who desert the ones they're supposed to love. Nobody should have to understand. I sure as hell never will.*

"So what do you say?" Mary asked. Her tone was colorless. "You want to go to the park and see if we can find anything out?"

"Yeah." Gaia nodded. So much for opening up and confiding. She felt nauseated. Trying to determine whether she had killed a drug dealer was far preferable to digging up more of her past. "I do."

Exquisite Skills

SUBJECT: JOHN DOE, MALE, CAUCASIAN, AGED forty to fifty. Admitted to St. Vincent's at 10:33 P.M. December 28. Injuries: fractured clavicle, fractured jaw, massive internal bleeding. Preliminary reports indicate assault. Subject is still unconscious. Condition is stable but critical. Fourteen grams of cocaine were discovered on his person.

Loki tossed the report on his desk without bothering to read the rest. There was no point. It merely confirmed what he had witnessed with his own eyes.

He'd been wrong to doubt Gaia's discipline. Very wrong. A smile spread across his face as he leaned back in his leather chair, basking in the sunshine that streamed through the giant windows of the loft. He didn't understand why Ella was upset. She stood by the door, pacing the wooden floor in small circles. But then, the woman's motives almost always defied logic.

"She could have killed him," Ella muttered.

"I'd have been that much more impressed if she had," Loki replied dryly. "And he still might die. He's not out of the woods yet."

Ella stopped pacing and shot Loki a hard stare. "She's out of control. If she had—"

"On the contrary," he interrupted, glaring at her. "She's very much *in* control. Had you been there with me, you would know. Her skills are still exquisite." He paused for a moment, furrowing his brow. "And why *weren't* you there, exactly?"

"I'm married," Ella snapped. She looked down at the floor. "In case you forgot, that takes up a lot of my time." Her voice softened. "George is a smart man. I've been playing this charade for five years, and if—"

"You're complaining?" Loki demanded.

Ella lifted her eyes. Her jaw twitched.

"Because if you're not satisfied, I can simply have

you removed from the assignment," he remarked. His tone was casual.

She didn't answer. Loki smiled again. Every operative knew what it meant to be removed from an assignment. It meant removal from existence. `Permanently.` She would envy "John Doe" in her final breathing moments.

"All I'm saying is that her behavior has been erratic," Ella murmured after a moment. "You said so yourself. One day she's out vandalizing, the next she nearly kills someone."

Loki shrugged. "I know now that it shows she has a highly developed sense of loyalty. All we have to do is manipulate that loyalty when the time comes."

Ella threw her hands in the air. "Well, when *is* that time?" she cried. "We've been—"

"That's none of your concern," Loki interrupted. "You *know* that. And if anyone's behavior has been erratic, it's been yours."

Again she was silent.

Loki's eyes fell back to the report. With the drug dealer out of commission—indefinitely, it seemed—Mary Moss's life was no longer in jeopardy. They would have to come up with an alternate plan should it become necessary that she be neutralized. But he needed to observe her a few more times before he made that decision. It would have to be made soon, though. Ella's impatience notwithstanding, time was getting shorter.

Yes. The new year would bring many changes. For Gaia most of all.

Ella placed her hands on the back of Loki's neck. "I'm tired of waiting. And I'm tired of watching," she whispered, rubbing his shoulders—at first tentatively . . . but then slowly, sensuously.

"Most of all, I'm tired of not getting what I want. What I know you want, too." She leaned down and kissed his lips softly, stroking his cheek.

For a moment Loki let himself be kissed. It had been a long time. Too long.

He pulled her onto his lap, caressing the small of her back with one hand. With the other he pulled at a strand of her hair. For such an incredible bitch she could be so soft, so delicious, so . . .

Suddenly his senses returned in a blinding flash. What the hell was he doing? He had no time for Ella's foolishness. Loki stood abruptly, dumping Ella into a pitiful heap. He met her eyes with a glare of disgust. After all of the mistakes he had made, how could he ever be willing to let a woman distract him from the task at hand? Especially an inferior specimen like Ella. He knew perfectly well who she could never be. And so did she.

Neither of them had any illusions about that.

Too Damn Pitiful

FOUR DAYS. THAT WAS THE LONGEST ED had ever gone without talking to Gaia. But even *that* seemed like nothing compared to the past two. Of course, the queasiness probably had something to with it. And the terrible certainty that the two days would stretch to three, then to four . . . and that he might not ever talk to her again.

But he'd made a decision. He didn't care what happened to Gaia Moore. Not as long as she insisted on `acting like an imbecile`. He wouldn't apologize.

Funny how those kinds of decisions never seemed to stick.

He sat at his desk, staring at his computer. He couldn't bring himself to do anything else. Like turn *on* the computer. He thought about calling Heather, mostly to see Phoebe . . . but she would probably be on her way out to have some fun somewhere, and that would just make him *more* depressed. Anyway, if Heather *or* Phoebe wanted to hang out with him, they would call him. And they hadn't. Seeing him at that diner had probably been enough Ed Fargo to last the Gannis sisters another few years or so—

Stop feeling so goddamned sorry for yourself.

He ground his teeth. All day he'd sat in this exact spot, staring at his distorted reflection in the grayish cube of the blank screen, reliving the events of that night in Chinatown. He couldn't even remember how the fight with Gaia had started. One minute they were staring at a rack of grade F meat; the next, he was storming away from her.

Why? What the hell had she done to piss him off so much?

If anything, *he* should call to apologize. He was the one who had freaked out. He'd been so damn jumpy. For no reason at all, really. Now that he thought about it, he probably had imagined seeing that fat bearded guy in the window. And even if he hadn't, that guy wouldn't have tried anything on a crowded street.

And even if that fat guy *had* tried something—even if by some miracle that guy had suddenly attacked all three of them with a machete or a submachine gun . . . then Gaia would have kicked his ass.

Ed shook his head.

He was to blame. There was a way to end his suffering, though. Several, actually. Turn on the computer. Pick up the phone. Call. E-mail. Apologize. Bada-bing, bada-boom. Over. Problem solved.

But he just couldn't bring himself to do it. Because deep down in his battered soul, a part of him still clung to his old pride—the pride he'd felt when he could walk, when he was known as "Shred," the baddest skater south of Fourteenth Street. It would be just too damn pitiful if he made the first move to reconcile with Gaia. Yes. If she valued the friendship as much as he did, *she* would have to be the one to call. It was a test. And if she failed—

Bzzzzzt.

Ed jumped slightly. The apartment buzzer was ringing. He rolled his eyes and scooted out of his bedroom into the narrow hall that led to the entranceway. It was probably some guy from Federal Express, delivering a lame Christmas fruit basket from a cousin twice removed in Hackensack that Ed had met only once.

He pressed the intercom button. "Hello?"

There was a crackle of static. "Ed?"

His jaw dropped. That voice. It sounded like . . . *her*.

"Gaia?" he asked, pressing the button again.

"Yeah. Is it cool if I come up?"

"Uh . . . sure."

His arm fell to his side. He glanced around the apartment. His heart immediately started thumping. Gaia Moore was coming up. *Here.*

Maybe he should clean up a little bit. Maybe he should tear down all the Christmas streamers and bulbs and paper angels that were still strewn all over the place. Jeez. He never realized how lame they were. This place was like one giant advertisement for corporate holidays. Speaking of which, at least his parents were at work. That lowered the lameness factor considerably—

He scowled.

Why was he getting so worked up? Almost

everyone had Christmas decorations, or Hanukkah decorations, or Kwanza decorations . . . probably even Gaia's mysterious guardians. There was no point in trying to mask the fact that his parents weren't hip. Ed rubbed his palms on his jeans. He'd never tried to put on an act with Gaia before. He shouldn't start now. . . .

The doorbell rang.

He took a deep breath. Then he rolled over and opened the door.

Gaia stood before him. She didn't come in. She looked more beautiful than ever. But he didn't know why; she was still wearing those baggy cargo pants, some nondescript gray sweatshirt, and that overcoat-and-hat combo that looked like it had been swiped off a homeless person. Maybe it was her hair. It looked more sultry somehow—hanging in tousled curls across her face. And her cheeks were flushed from the cold, almost as if she were blushing.

"Hey, Ed. Sorry to bother you."

"I . . ." He didn't even know what he wanted to say.

"Look, I don't have a lot of time," Gaia said quickly. She stared down at her sneakers. "Mary's waiting downstairs. I just wanted to tell you that I'm really sorry about the way I acted the other night. It was stupid."

Ed just stared at her. He couldn't believe this. He

didn't have a clue as to how to respond. For once Gaia Moore was doing exactly what he'd prayed she would do. It was almost frightening.

She looked up at him. "You were right, too, by the way."

"What do you mean?"

"There was a guy following us. Mary's old drug dealer."

"*What?*" Ed gasped. "How do you—"

"Look, I can't go into it right now, okay?" she interrupted. She glanced back toward the elevator and flashed him a quick, enigmatic smile. "Just . . . things are a little weird right now. But I just want you to know that I'm sorry. I swear I've learned my lesson this time. Okay?"

He nodded vigorously. "Well, yeah. I mean, I'm sorry, too—"

"I gotta go. See ya." She turned back down the hall.

Ed blinked. But before he could even open his mouth, he heard the elevator bell ring, then the doors open and shut.

He laughed. Well. It looked like everything was back to normal. He was friends with her again, and she was involved in something bad again. Yup. It was just another ordinary day for her. Appear out of nowhere, make Ed experience a dozen emotions in the space of about thirty seconds, and vanish. Classic Gaia.

"OH, NO," MARY CROAKED THE MOMENT
she and Gaia turned onto
MacDougal Street. She pointed
a shaky finger at the park.

Turf War

Gaia peered through the tree
branches, following Mary's outstretched arm—
straight to the spot where she had left Skizz on the
ground.

Her mind suddenly went blank. She knew why. She
should have been scared.

Cops were there.

Part of the path had been roped off with yellow
police tape. Two policemen in dark blue jackets were
standing on the other side of it, talking to two guys in
long trench coats—detectives, maybe. One of them
had a camera.

"He must have died," Mary whispered, shivering in
the cold. "He must have—"

"Shhh," Gaia whispered gently. She knew she
should probably turn and run—but instead she felt
only a powerful curiosity. The presence of cops was
actually a *good* thing. Now there was a quick way to
find out if Skizz had died there last night. She knew
police procedure when a body was found in the park.
Her face darkened. Oh, yes. She knew it all too well.
When "the Gentleman" had murdered Cassie
Greenman there a couple of months ago (and tried to
make Gaia his next victim), the police had outlined

166

Cassie's body in chalk on the ground, leaving a grim memory of the crime for all to see. So if Gaia had really killed Skizz, there ought to be one of those outlines as well.

"Wait here," Gaia instructed Mary. "I'm gonna go check it out—"

"Are you crazy?" Mary hissed. "Gaia, they could be looking for you."

She shrugged. "Then there's no point in postponing the inevitable, right? I might as well get it over with. Just hang out here. If you see me getting arrested or something, take off." She turned and hurried across the street without waiting for Mary to reply.

Hopefully Mary would follow her advice. Gaia figured she would. After all, Mary had something working in her favor that Gaia didn't. Fear.

Gaia's eyes narrowed as she entered the park. The glare of the winter sunshine made it difficult to see, but from what she could tell . . . no, there definitely wasn't any sort of chalk drawing on the ground. A good sign. Of course, Skizz could have died at the hospital—

"Can I help you, miss?" one of the cops asked as she approached.

She smiled at him innocently. "I was just wondering what was going on."

"Nothing," the other cop replied shortly. "Just move along."

"Did . . . uh, did somebody die?" she asked, staring

down at the marked-off area. Several large, rust-colored stains glistened on the pavement.

"Somebody was assaulted," the first cop said. His voice hardened. "Now, please move along. This is a crime scene."

Gaia nodded, then turned away. So Skizz might still be alive. Assault wasn't murder. She glanced surreptitiously back at MacDougal Street. Mary was still standing on the corner, staring at her. Gaia had started walking back toward the park exit when she heard a couple of footsteps behind her.

"Excuse me? Miss?"

The guy with the trench coat and camera was catching up with her. Now that he was closer, she could see that he didn't look like a typical cop. Hardly. He looked more like he belonged at some kind of pretentious gallery opening in SoHo. He was wearing a four-button suit under his coat, and he had a goatee. His black hair was slicked back with gunk.

"Yeah?" she asked.

He leaned close to her and gently took her elbow, steering her farther away from the crime scene. "My name's Jared Smith," he murmured. "I'm a reporter for *The Daily News.* Is it all right if I ask you a couple of questions?"

Gaia hesitated. She glanced back at Mary. Even from this distance Gaia could tell that Mary was getting more anxious by the second. She kept bouncing up and down on the balls of her feet. But this guy might know something about what happened—something that the cops weren't willing to share.

"I guess so," she mumbled. "What do you want to know?"

"Do you hang out here a lot? In the park, I mean?"

She took a step back, trying not to gag. His cologne reeked. "Um, sometimes," she answered. "Why?"

"Have you ever been offered drugs here?" he asked. He pulled a little notebook out of his trench coat pocket.

"No." Gaia scowled. "What's this about, anyway?"

"The cops think the assault might have been the result of a turf war in the drug trade," he said. He fished for a pencil, then gave her a quick, disdainful once-over. "I was just wondering if you knew anything about that."

Whoever this Jared Smith was, he sure as hell didn't have any manners. Just because she wasn't dressed as if she'd walked straight out of an Armani ad, he automatically assumed that she was a junkie. But at least she knew now that she wasn't a suspect. She supposed it made sense. Who would ever suspect a junkie of kicking a big fat drug dealer's ass?

"Can I ask you something?" she said.

He shrugged, jotting something down in his notebook.

"Is the victim alive?"

"Barely," he answered. "But he'll make it. He's at St. Vincent's. Apparently the cops have been looking for him. He's being arraigned today on three counts of possession with intent to sell, resisting arrest, and assault with a deadly. As soon as he's able, he's gonna be moved to the infirmary at Rikers Island. Why do you want to know? Was he your supplier?"

Gaia ignored the question. She resisted the temptation to punch him in the face. This smug bastard needed some major work on his people skills. Not that she was one to talk, of course. But she was glad to end this little interview. Skizz had survived— and it looked like he'd be getting locked away for a very long time. Mary's worries were over. And so were Gaia's. She felt like a tremendous weight had suddenly been lifted from her shoulders. She *wasn't* a killer. She might be a lot of other things . . . but she still wasn't that. She whirled and strode away from him.

"Hey!" he called after her. "I'm asking you a question!"

"He wasn't my supplier," she answered, without even bothering to look over her shoulder. She picked up her pace in case he tried to follow her.

"Can I get your name? In case I want to quote . . ."

The sound of his annoying voice was lost in her footsteps as she darted back across MacDougal Street to Mary.

"What's going on?" Mary whispered, peering behind Gaia at the park. "What did that guy want? Is he a detective—"

"There's nothing to worry about," Gaia interrupted gently. She grabbed Mary's arm and whisked her around the corner toward Sixth Avenue. "That guy was just some sleazebag reporter. But he told me that Skizz is on his way to jail. The cops think a rival dealer did it."

Mary blinked several times. She looked at Gaia, then stared down at her feet as they walked side by side. "Are you *serious?*"

"Yeah. He's wanted for, like, eight felonies or something."

"But . . . what if he tells the cops who kicked his ass?" Mary asked. She shook her head. "I mean, he can describe the way you look, you know?"

Gaia laughed. Funny. She hadn't even thought of that. But it didn't concern her very much—and not only because she was fearless. She doubted very much that Skizz would rat her out to the cops. He was probably scared shitless of her. And the cops probably wouldn't believe him, anyway. The idea of a seventeen-year-old girl's nearly killing an armed drug dealer was just too preposterous. At least, that was the way it had always worked in the past.

"I guess we'll just have to cross that bridge when we come to it," Gaia said, patting Mary's shoulder. "But for now, I'd say things are cool."

From: shred@alloymail.com
To: gaia13@alloymail.com
Re: 411
Time: 5:03 P.M.

Hey, G$—

   Very psyched you came by. I have to say, I'm a little curious about what you said. What did you mean by "things are a little weird"? Can you be more specific? I know you don't like answering these kinds of questions, but a little info would put my mind at ease. Also, what are you doing tomorrow night? I need to escape my family. Thanking you in advance—
   Ed

From: gaia13@alloymail.com
To: shred@alloymail.com
Re: No worries, no plans
Time: 6:00 P.M.

Hey, Ed—

   Forget about what I said. Things aren't going to get weird. As for tomorrow night, I have no plans. Mary and I were talking about watching TV at her house and stuffing our faces with ice cream. Yes, I know it's lame. But if you feel like being lame, too, consider this an invitation. We're going to get together around nine.

   G$

From: shred@alloymail.com
To: gaia13@alloymail.com
Re: Being lame
Time: 7:08 P.M.

Hey, G$—
   Count me in. I'll be there.

From: gaia13@alloymail.com
To: smoon@alloymail.com
Re: [no subject]
Time: 10:01 P.M.

Hi. I'm just writing to tell you that I think you're the biggest jerk I ever met and I can't believe you're back with Heather and I hate you and I never want to talk to you again. And everything I just wrote is a lie. I miss you. I want to call you, but I can't. I can't even bring myself to say your name out loud. I don't know why. I'm not scared of you. I don't get scared, in case you didn't know. I just feel confused. So is this what fear feels like? Can you tell me?

<<*DELETE*>>

He'd envisioned
making out
with Gaia
countless
times, in
thousands of **to**
different **gaia**
scenarios—but
never once had
he imagined
this.

Homecoming

TOM MOORE'S LEGS WERE PRACTICALLY NUMB.

They always went numb in airplanes, even in first-class seats. But his mind wasn't on his own discomfort. His fingers furiously flew across his laptop, searching the agency's databases for Loki's known associates. He'd been awake for almost thirty-six straight hours—and airborne for about half that time—but there was no chance he could sleep. Not until he figured out who had contacted him.

Search: Loki—U.S. Militia Groups.

No match found.

He shook his head. Nothing. Only when he searched for Loki's contacts outside the United States did he come up with any matches: the usual list of terrorists and arms dealers—shadowy characters from groups like Hammas and Shining Path. But the man who had called didn't have the slightest trace of an accent.

So who was he?

Tom rubbed his bloodshot eyes and leaned back in his chair, staring out the round window at a wall of blackness. The plane was somewhere over the Atlantic now. It would probably be touching down at JFK within the hour. He had to think. Who would Loki employ that could possibly have access to Gaia? One of her friends? Tom thought he knew them: There was that boy Sam and the kid in the wheelchair . . . and that was pretty much it. For the most part Gaia kept to herself. And there was no way either of *them* could be working for Loki. So was it somebody whom Gaia had met recently?

He hunched back over the screen and typed for what must have been the hundredth time:

Search: Loki—recent communications

The computer hummed for a split second.

2 matches found.

ELJ (identity unknown)

BFF (identity unknown)

He kept coming up with the same two sets of initials over and over again. And he had no idea who either "ELJ" or "BFF" could possibly be. Neither did the agency, apparently. It was a miracle they had found out *that* much. Loki was meticulous in covering his tracks.

Tom's eyes wandered to the window again. There was a possibility, of course, that he hadn't allowed himself to consider.

It was a very obvious possibility. A *probability*, in fact—which was that the call was a trap. Loki might have even made the call himself, masking the timbre of his voice with an electronic device. Loki might well have wanted to lure Tom out of Russia in order to dispose of him once and for all, so that there would be nothing standing between Loki and his twin brother's daughter. . . .

Tom slammed the laptop shut. Speculation was a

waste of time. He'd know the answers to all these questions soon enough.

Loki might answer them himself.

A Toast

"ELLA, HONEY?" GEORGE CALLED FROM THE living room. "Don't you want some wine? I'm just about to crack open another bottle."

Better make that two, Ella thought, groaning silently. She sat at the kitchen table, feeling very much as if her life were draining from her body. What the hell was she even doing here? It was two nights before New Year's Eve, for God's sake. The best time of year for parties. The big end-of-the-year blitz. Almost everyone they knew was out on the town. Yet George had insisted on staying at home every single night since Christmas. Socializing with other people was the only remotely tolerable aspect of their sham marriage—but they didn't even have any plans for New Year's Eve itself. Did the old man really believe she *wanted* to be alone with him? Was he really that blind?

Yes. He was. She found herself smiling in spite of her anger. He was that blind because she was such an excellent actress.

"El-la!" he called in a singsong voice.

"Coming!" she answered with false brightness.

He was so goddamned cheerful. She thought of the thirty-eight-caliber pistol hidden behind her night table. It would be so easy to run upstairs and grab it. So easy to twist on the silencer. So easy to shut him up for good. On these nights— the painful, romantic nights, the nights when she had to play the role of a loving wife . . . well, she couldn't take them much longer. The years were beginning to take their toll. No payoff could be worth this agony.

She swallowed. No. The payoff *would* be worth it. She would make sure of it. And it would far exceed anything that Loki had envisioned for her. Oh, yes. In fact, her reward would include Loki himself.

Ella took a deep breath and plastered a smile on her face, then pushed herself from the table and strode into the living room.

"There you are," George murmured. He was leaning back on the sofa, struggling with a corkscrew and a glistening green bottle. At least she lived luxuriously. In a purely materialistic sense, she had everything she needed. For the time being, anyway. That bottle of chardonnay probably cost seventy bucks. Two crystal glasses sat on the mahogany coffee table. Those weren't cheap, either. Wedding presents. How ironic. The logs burning in the fireplace cast the room in a soft glow; few brownstones in New York had real working fireplaces. Her life was good. She should just enjoy it while it lasted.

Pop!

"There we go," George whispered. He laid the corkscrew on the table, then filled her glass with the golden liquid.

"Thank you," Ella murmured seductively. She raised her glass as George filled his own. "Cheers."

He put down the bottle and lifted his glass. "Cheers." He leaned forward, then hesitated. "Wait. I want to ask you a question. Do you have any New Year's resolutions?"

She smirked. "It's not even New Year's Eve."

"I know, but I guess I've been thinking a lot these days about the changes I'd like to make. So?" His smile widened. "What's it going to be?"

"Well . . ." She edged closer to him. "The only change I'd like to make is to spend more time with my loving and very sexy husband," she whispered. He blushed slightly, as she knew he would. It was so easy to control him. "How about you?"

His face grew serious for a moment. "I want to make sure that Gaia is happy. I want to include her more. To really make her feel like part of the family."

Ella nodded. How sweet. And pathetic. And infuriating. It was almost too much. The mere mention of Gaia's name made her insides twist. But her smile didn't falter. She tilted her glass. "A toast. To Gaia."

"To Gaia," George echoed, tapping her glass with his own.

Yes, Ella thought. May she rot in hell.

THE WEEK BETWEEN CHRISTMAS AND

New Year's Eve was Sam's least favorite time of the year—at least when he was in New York. True, he'd been here only once in the past: last year. But he already knew the score. Inevitably the entire week meant going from one lame party to the next, night after night, always try-ing to track down an elusive great time that never ma-terialized—and winding up each time on the street at 3 A.M., freezing, disappointed, and trying to hail a cab back home.

The Score

Clearly tonight would be no exception.

For starters, he didn't even know where he *was*. Well, he knew he was at some filthy, cramped apart-ment in the East Village—but he had no idea who lived here. Kelly? Christie? Something like that. Whoever she was, she loved red lights and deafening industrial rock and was a friend of a friend of Heather's sister Phoebe . . . and she'd offered some kind of incomprehensible greeting when he and

Heather and Phoebe walked through the door. "Welcome, warriors." At least that was what he thought she'd said. Whatever the hell that was supposed to mean. And then she'd disappeared.

So now he found himself drinking a warm beer and wondering where his girlfriend and her sister went. What a blast. Whoopee. He tried to maneuver his way from the tiny living room to the hall by the closet-sized kitchen—but just ended up getting mushed against a wall by a group of heavily pierced strangers. They were all dressed in black. The wall vibrated in time to the music. He scowled and slurped down his beer. Best just to get drunk. At least he'd be able to forget—

"Sam! *There* you are!"

Phoebe was jumping up and down by the kitchen doorway, trying to make eye contact with him. She waved her hands over the heads of the mob.

"Come here!" she called.

Yeah, right. She was only about ten feet away, but he'd need a battering ram to reach her. He shrugged and tried to smile.

"Hold on a sec," Phoebe shouted. "We're coming out. . . ." Her voice was lost in the din as she ducked back into the kitchen.

Good luck, he thought. He drained the rest of the beer in one long gulp. *Blech.* He made a face and wiped his mouth with his sleeve—but a pleasant, warm numbness began to spread from his stomach through-out his body. Hopefully if Heather and Phoebe *did* make it out of the kitchen, they'd bring him another drink. It was strange. Usually he wasn't a huge fan of booze. It just made his head swim. It probably made him act a lot more obnoxious, too. A lot of kids in his dorm drank all the time, and if they were any indication of how people acted when they were drunk—

He stiffened. His eyes zeroed in on a tall girl coming out of the kitchen.

Her back was turned to him, but from here it definitely looked like Gaia.

Yes. That hair. That long, blond tangle. Nobody had hair like that. He stood on his tiptoes. His heart began to race. What was she doing here? What . . .

The girl glanced over her shoulder.

Shit. Excitement fizzled out of him like air hissing from a deflating flat tire. Apparently somebody else *did* have hair like that. Somebody a lot less attractive.

He shook his head. Of course Gaia wouldn't come to the same party. And even if she *had,* he would have nothing to say to her. He suddenly found he was ex-tremely pissed off. At everyone. At Heather and Phoebe for bringing him here. At the people in this room. But most of all at Gaia—for dropping off the face of the earth, for finding a new boyfriend, and for dominating his thoughts about ninety-five percent of the time when he *should* be in love with someone else. . . .

"Whoa!" Heather's familiar shriek tore through the crowd. He couldn't see her, but she was obviously close by. He shook his head again, overcome with guilt. What the hell was his problem? He *was* in love with her. Heather was beautiful. Heather was smart. Heather had a cool sister who was *also* beautiful. She was everything a guy could want—

"Excuse me! Sorry!"

A second later Heather burst from between two spaced-out-looking grunge types and nearly fell against Sam. She clutched a plastic cup of beer in each hand. A couple of drops splashed on Sam's flannel shirt.

"Whoops," she murmured, giggling. She handed Sam one of the cups, then used her free hand to try to wipe his shirt. She swayed slightly. Her face was flushed. "Sorry about that. It's just kinda hard to move around in here."

"No kidding," he said.

She took a huge gulp of beer.

"Maybe you've had enough," he muttered.

"Oh, come on." She slapped his arm. Her eyes were heavily lidded. "It's a party. You know, the last time I was this messed up . . ." She didn't finish. Her gaze became glassy.

"*What?*" Sam demanded impatiently.

She sighed and shook her head. "Never mind." She smiled up at him. "Iss not worth getting into," she slurred. "So are you having fun?"

"The time of my life," he stated flatly.

"Good." She nodded, somehow oblivious to the biting sarcasm in his voice.

"So where's Phoebe?" he asked, struggling to keep a lid on his annoyance.

Heather shrugged dramatically. "Who knows? She's a . . . she's a free spirit." She burst out laughing, as if that were the funniest joke anyone had ever made.

That was it. Something snapped. He didn't know what it was. Maybe it was Heather's drunkenness, or the crowd, or the stale stink of beer . . . but he'd had enough. He brushed past her and tried to force his way to the door.

"Hey!" she cried, still laughing. She grabbed his shoulder from behind. "What's wrong?"

"Nothing," he muttered, shoving through the grunge kids. "I just want to go home."

"What?" she yelled. "I can't hear you—"

"I want to go *home*," he snapped, turning back around.

She blinked. Then she raised her hands, grinning crookedly. "All right, all right," she said. "Whew. No need to yell. Lemme just get my coat. I'll tell Phoebe we're leaving. This party's kind of lame, anyway."

He opened his mouth—but before he could say anything, she stepped past him and snaked her way into the kitchen. He was going to tell her that she should just stay here, that he didn't want to ruin her good time, that he was just feeling lousy . . . but those all would have been lies. The truth was that he didn't want to be with her. No matter *where* they were. Not tonight. He wanted to be with someone else.

But it was too late. His girlfriend was coming with him.

He eyed his beer, then lifted the cup and started chugging. Best just to go numb, right?

GAIA STARED DOWN AT THE BOTTOM OF the empty pint of chocolate chocolate chip ice cream.

The Antidote

"No more." She groaned.

She couldn't believe she'd eaten the whole thing—on top of another pint before that *plus* an amazing dinner (chicken Kiev, care of the Moss's Russian cook, Olga). . . . Her stomach felt like it was about to explode. She glanced up at Mary and Ed. They weren't faring much better. Mary was sprawled on the living-room couch beside her, clutching her belly. Ed was slumped in his wheelchair in front of the flickering, muted television set. He frowned at his own half-eaten bowl of Rocky Road. He looked a little pale.

"I don't know if I can finish this," he said blankly.

"Hey, kids!" Mary's mother called from the kitchen. "Do you want some more ice cream?"

Mary rolled her eyes. "Uh . . . no, thanks, Mom."

Gaia exchanged a quick glance with Ed. The two of them burst out laughing. Gaia winced. She placed her own empty carton next to Ed's bowl and held her sides.

"Stop it," she moaned. "Don't make me laugh. I'm too full."

"How about a little more chicken, dear?" Ed asked, imitating Mary's mom.

"Stop it!" Gaia closed her eyes for a moment and shook her head, giggling. "I mean it. It's not funny. . . ."

"Hey, check it out," Ed suddenly announced, pointing at the TV screen. "They're talking about all the preparations for New Year's Eve in Times Square." He snorted. "You know, I've lived in New York my whole life, but I've never gotten the whole Times Square thing. Who would actually want to *go* there? I mean, who would want to stand out in the freezing cold in Midtown, packed in like sardines with a bunch of strangers, just to watch some cheesy ball drop?"

"To be part of history, Ed," Mary answered dryly.

Gaia smirked. She didn't get it, either. She'd read somewhere that something like a million and a half people had gone there last year. And they had all been stuffed into an eight-block radius. How could they even *breathe*? She had no desire to experience New Year's Eve like that. Nope. She wanted to be someplace like this. Sitting in a cozy apartment, enjoying the company of friends . . . yes. This was perfect. This was right.

All at once Gaia felt a lump forming in her throat—the same lump she felt a few days ago on the subway with Mary. *Oh, Jesus.* She wasn't going to get all weepy and sentimental again, was she? It was not good form. Not for a superbadass chick like Gaia Moore. But she couldn't help it. She hadn't been so content or relaxed since . . . well, since she'd had a real family.

She swallowed.

A real family. The words rang through her mind like the distant cry of some tortured animal. She shook her head. She wasn't going to think about her mother or father. Not anymore. She wasn't going to think about love lost or love turned to hate. None of that mattered anymore. *This* was her family now: Mary and Ed. They were all she needed.

"You know what's even more pathetic than watching New Year's Eve celebrations at home?" Ed asked with a grin. "Watching the *preparations* for New Year's Eve celebrations."

Gaia smiled and turned her attention to the TV screen. There was no need to dwell on the past. It was best just to have a good time. The camera panned up from the streets to the darkened crystal sphere, hovering on a long cord over Times Square. It looked like a giant disco ball. All those people would gather to see *that*? She sighed. Ed was right: It *was* kind of pathetic watching this stuff. Besides, New Year's Eve really didn't mean anything at all. The end of the year was a totally arbitrary date. If they had been using the Chinese calendar, December 31 would be just another day.

"Oh, by the way," Ed said. "I want to take this opportunity to let you both know that I think you're the biggest losers on the planet."

Gaia kicked the back of his wheelchair.

"Hey!" He chuckled.

"How about some cookies?" Mrs. Moss called.

"Mom!" Mary yelled, grimacing.

Ed started cracking up again. "So . . ." He grabbed the remote and clicked off the television, then turned his wheelchair around so that he was facing the two of them. "If we aren't gonna eat cookies, what *are* we gonna do?"

Mary raised her eyebrows. "You know, we never got a chance to finish the game."

"What game?" Ed asked.

Gaia laughed. It figured Ed wouldn't remember. "What do you think, you dope?" she asked. "Truth or dare."

Ed frowned. Then he laughed, too. He slumped deep into his chair, burying his face in his hands and shaking his head. "That's what I get for opening my big mouth. . . ."

"Look, Ed, we won't leave the apartment this time, all right?" Mary said. "It'll be strictly indoors. It's too cold, and we're all too full—"

"But I thought the game was over," Ed interrupted.

He looked up. "Besides, isn't it customary that a game of spin the bottle always follows a game of truth or dare?"

"Where?" Mary asked dryly. "In Fargoland?"

Ed shrugged and smiled. "Hey, I'm just trying to liven things up a little bit."

"So whose turn is it?" Gaia asked, suddenly excited. *This* was the good time she'd been looking for—the antidote to thinking about all the crap in her life.

Mary smirked at her. "Are you volunteering?"

Gaia nodded and sat up straight. "You got it."

"Okay." Mary leaned back. She looked very pleased with herself. "I think I've got a dare that'll liven things up Fargo style. Gaia?" She paused dramatically. "I dare you to make out with Ed."

For a moment Gaia was stunned into silence. She could feel a flush creeping up her cheeks. This was certainly something she hadn't expected. But then again, she should have expected no less from Mary Moss.

"That's it?" Gaia asked, filling her voice with bravado. Jeez. Did Mary think that kissing Ed was some kind of big deal? It was like kissing a brother, if she'd *had* a brother. . . . She glanced over at him.

Okay, not *quite* like kissing a brother. Gaia had to admit it, Ed was actually a *guy*. Her friend, yes. A complete freak sometimes. But a *guy*. And when it came to kissing guys, her track record was pretty lousy.

Gaia roused herself out of her thoughts long enough

to notice that Ed was scowling at Mary. For some reason, it sent a small pain stabbing into her chest.

"You scared or something?" she asked him, pretending to be offended.

ED COULDN'T ANSWER THE QUESTION. He couldn't answer it because he *was* scared. And ashamed. And a little crest-fallen, too. He'd envisioned making out **Ready** with Gaia countless times, in thousands of different scenarios—but never once had he imagined *this*: exchanging a few sloppy kisses for Mary Moss's benefit. On the other hand...

Gaia winked at him. At first he thought she'd seemed a little shocked, but it must have been his imagination. Gaia looked completely unruffled as always. "You ready, baby?" she mock whispered.

He barely heard the question. His heart was thumping so fast that the sound of his pulse filled his ears; he felt almost like he was buried under a thick, gauzy blanket. He no longer felt uncomfortably full, either. His stomach felt strangely empty. Regardless of whether or not this moment conformed to any fantasies he'd had, he realized that it was actually happening.

He was about to kiss Gaia Moore.

He really was. He gaped at her as she approached the wheelchair. Events unfolded way too fast when Gaia got together with Mary. One second he was watching TV; the next—

"And when I say make out, I mean make out," Mary said, giggling. "No half-assed, closed-mouthed smooching."

"I know," Gaia murmured. She stood in between his legs and leaned over him, gripping the wheelchair's hand rests to steady herself. Her face was now barely three inches from his own. He could see every detail of her porcelain skin, every fleck in her blue eyes. . . . He could even detect a slight tremble in her lips. He couldn't believe how soft they looked, how moist, how . . .

"Uh, you sure you want to do this?" he asked, swallowing.

Instead of answering, she simply covered his lips with her own.

GAIA FELT LIKE SHE WAS FLOATING. HER eyes were closed. Her lips felt the

Turn-On

texture of Ed's lips; her tongue explored his mouth. For the first few seconds the motions were mechanical. Her body was acting independently of her thoughts. Her mind drifted back through all the kisses she'd experienced in the past. But then, without warning, she shifted back to the present.

She was enjoying this.

The way Ed kissed her . . . it was *tender* somehow. Caring. Loving. Sensual.

Did Ed feel the same way? She couldn't help but wonder what he was thinking. And then she stopped wondering. She forgot about Mary. She forgot about everything.

Ed's fingers brushed against her arm.

A little tingle raced down her spine.

Whoa. What was going on here?

She *was* enjoying this. She tentatively let her fingers travel to his soft, thick hair, noticing that his hands had moved to her lower back. The sensation it caused was dizzying.

Without thinking, she pressed her body toward him. She wanted to stretch the moment as long as it would go. Ed responded, pulling her closer to him and pressing his lips more urgently onto her own. This was insane.

Suddenly Gaia was hit with the urge to pull back. She wanted to see Ed. She wanted to know what was going on in his head. She jerked away abruptly, meeting his eyes with her own baffled gaze. His face was flushed. He held Gaia's stare in a look that seemed half pain, half elation.

"Ooh, baby!" Mary cried.

And that was it.

The moment was shattered. Gaia was no longer in a private little world of two; she was back in Mary Moss's apartment, playing truth or dare. She backed away and took a deep breath. Her heart was fluttering.

Ed didn't speak. Their eyes met for a moment.

Whew. Gaia smiled. That was weird. Her feelings of a second before seemed to be floating away—like a wisp of smoke from a candle. It was formless and intangible . . . and then it was gone. What had she been thinking? This was *Ed*. Her friend. She laughed and took a deep breath. It was a good thing it was someone else's turn now.

"So, Ed," she managed to say nonchalantly. "Was it as good for you as it was for me?"

That had been
quite an
enlightening
little exchange.
Quite an
outpouring **the**
of **decision**
emotion. Two
girls,
united by
loneliness . . .

THE NIGHT COULD BE WORSE, ED REALIZED.
It could be a hell of a lot worse.

Lie or Dare

True, he was playing the annoying game again. But on the plus side he'd eaten a great meal. And he was hanging out in a hot girl's living room. And it looked like he was going to be spending the night here. It was already almost one o'clock.

Oh, yeah. He'd also kissed Gaia Moore.

That minor little thing. The thing that would explain why his heart was about to explode out of his chest. The thing that would explain why he could hardly breathe.

The weirdest part of it was that the memory was already fuzzy. It had happened only seconds ago, but it felt like a dream. Of course, he hadn't seen anything; his eyes had been closed. The only part of it that was clear was the sensation of her lips against his.

And that had been pretty nice. Pretty damn nice.

He shifted in his wheelchair and gazed at Gaia, stretched out on the couch beside Mary.

Yes. It *had* been nice. Hadn't it?

So why did Gaia look totally unaffected—as if nothing had happened at all? Hadn't she felt *anything*? She had pretty much initiated it by volunteering. . . .

Then he remembered. It was part of a game.

Right. A joke. Nothing more than that. A little comedy routine between friends. Actually, in a way, the kiss had been pretty symbolic of the way Gaia felt about him. She liked to push him. She liked to get him riled up. But only to make him laugh. In her eyes, he was the funny guy. The sidekick. Somebody whom she loved and wanted around—but not somebody she would ever take seriously, at least in a romantic way. That was why she had gone so far. She never would have kissed Sam Moon like that. Not in a game, anyway.

No silly dares or pranks or stunts would ever change the way she felt.

And the truly ironic (meaning shitty) thing was that she had no idea that he didn't *like* being the sidekick. She had no idea that he wanted something more out of their relationship. So. When he looked at it from that point of view, the kiss had sucked. But everything sucked from a certain point of view. What else was new?

"All right, Ed," Gaia said. "Your turn. You've ducked this for way too long. Truth or dare?"

He thought for a second. He could feel a sour mood creeping up on him, but he fought it back. He'd been having a lot of fun up until this point—and he wasn't going to let *his* problems ruin *their* good time. It wasn't Gaia's fault that she wasn't head over heels in love with him.

"Truth," he said.

Mary leaned over and whispered something in Gaia's ear. The two of them giggled.

Uh-oh. Ed's face grew hot.

"Good," Gaia said. She sat up straight. "If you could have sex with anyone in the world right now, who would it be? And it has to be somebody you actually know. Not a supermodel or Madonna or anything like that."

Ed stared back at her. *You, you moron,* he felt like shouting. But there was no point. She was smiling— mischievously, of course, but innocently, too. And he could see it in her beautiful blue eyes: She honestly didn't know that she was the only one he would *ever* want to have sex with . . . in a real kind of way. Even after that kiss, she had no idea. Of course, he'd be happy to have sex with a number of other girls in a not so real way, but it wasn't the same.

There was no way he could tell her. He'd known this all along, but only now did he really see *why* he couldn't confess his love for Gaia Moore. It wasn't the fear of rejection. He could live with rejection.

It was because he knew he'd hurt her.

If she found out how he really felt, she'd be horrified. On a variety of levels, too. One, because their relationship would never be the same; two, because she would realize that she was causing him pain; three, because there would be no way she would ever reciprocate. . . .

"There is someone," he found himself saying.

"Really?" Gaia's eyes widened. She leaned forward. "Who?"

Mary bolted upright beside her. "Yeah," she said eagerly. "Who?"

"You . . . you'll probably think it's a little weird," he said, swallowing. His pulse picked up a beat. It would be so easy to tell the truth. So easy to get it off his shoulders once and for all—

"That's okay," Gaia prodded. "Weird is good. So?"

"Phoebe Gannis," he said.

The name just popped into his head; he hadn't even been sure he was really going to say it until he uttered the words.

Gaia's face soured. "*Who?*"

"Heather's sister?" Mary asked. She smiled, cocking her eyebrow. "Jeez, Ed . . . I hope Heather didn't know about that while you two were dating."

Ed shrugged. In a way, his answer hadn't been a complete lie. He'd always had a little crush on Phoebe. And it had definitely been at its height while he was seeing Heather.

"Wait a second," Gaia said, raising her hands and glancing between Ed and Mary. Her brow was tightly furrowed. "Heather Gannis has a *sister?* How come I didn't know about this?"

"She has two, actually. Phoebe goes to college upstate," Ed said. "She's never around."

Gaia frowned. "Is Phoebe . . . Does she look like Heather?"

Ed allowed himself a little smile. He was almost

certain that Gaia was going to ask: *Is she pretty?* But that would mean acknowledging that Heather was pretty, and Gaia hated giving Heather any compliments—even indirectly. She was jealous of the girl. She had good reason, obviously; Heather was dating the guy of her dreams. But it was nice to know that Gaia occasionally experienced the same kinds of emotions as everyone else. Ed sometimes had a hard time remembering that.

"She's a lot better looking," he said. That wasn't a lie, either.

Mary laughed. "This is *very* interesting. You know, Ed—"

"Oh my God!" He slapped his forehead. "I totally forgot. My mom told me I *have* to come home tonight because we're having my grandparents over tomorrow." He turned and rolled over toward the door. *Now* he was lying. But they didn't have to know that. He was starting to realize that he'd been wrong about this night from the start. It would suck to spend the night here. He wouldn't be able to get any sleep. He'd just lie awake, thinking about Gaia. So tantalizingly close. Forget it. No way. He'd been through enough emotional crap already. "I'm really sorry—"

"But it's almost one o'clock," Gaia protested. "How are you gonna get home?"

"There are tons of cabs," he said, grabbing the doorknob. "It'll be no problem. Don't worry." He smiled over his shoulder. "You guys have fun, all right?"

Mary and Gaia glanced at each other.

"Uh . . . all right," Gaia said reluctantly. "But it's not the same without you."

He smirked. "I'm sure you'll figure out a way to make up for my absence," he said. He turned and headed into the hall. "See you later."

"Be safe," they called at the same time.

"You too," he said.

Amazingly, he felt pretty good as he rolled through the silent, darkened apartment to the front door. Weird. Things really *could* be worse. He had two good friends. Friends who actually saw past his wheelchair to the person sitting in it. How many people in his situation could say that? And so what if one of them drove him crazy? So what if he would always be in love with her? Being the sidekick wasn't *all* bad. No.

The world wasn't perfect, as he well knew. Far from it.

"SO IT LOOKS LIKE IT'S JUST YOU AND ME again," Gaia said with a sigh.

Mary settled in against the opposite end of the couch. "I guess so," she murmured. She was bummed to see Ed go. For the first time in a long while, she felt

Demons

like she'd made a breakthrough with him—like she was actually hanging around with Ed Fargo, her *friend*. As opposed to the sad guy who'd suffered a terrible accident. As opposed to the guy whom she pitied but wanted to avoid. And she knew that Gaia was to thank for the change. Gaia was so comfortable and easygoing with him that Mary just couldn't help being that way, too. And it wasn't even an act. She honestly hadn't thought of his wheelchair once.

On the other hand, Ed hated truth or dare. Mary grinned. There was no denying it: The game was a lot more fun when he wasn't around.

"Does that mean it's your turn?" Gaia asked.

"Yeah."

"So?" Gaia turned on her side, propping her head up with her elbow. She smiled. "Truth or dare?"

"I know if I pick dare, you're gonna make me eat another pint of ice cream or something. So I gotta go with truth."

Gaia nodded, but her eyes suddenly grew serious. "All right. Truth." She hesitated for a few seconds. "Why do you think you got addicted to coke?"

Mary blinked. Jesus. *That* wasn't the question she'd been expecting. It wasn't exactly in the madcap spirit of New Year's Eve fun. Mary had been thinking more along the lines of: Are you a virgin? What's the most disgusting thing you've ever done with a guy? Et cetera, et cetera. *Girlie* stuff. The kind of stuff you giggled about at 1 A.M., lying in bed with your best friend.

But then again, if Mary revealed something personal about herself, then Gaia would be more inclined to do the same. Yes. She could use this truth to her advantage. Besides, her therapist had told her that it was a good idea to talk about her drug experiences. The more she articulated her feelings, the more she opened up about her past—the less she would be inclined to keep her emotions bottled up inside her and find an unhealthy outlet for them. Anyway, it might be nice to share this stuff with a *friend* for once—instead of some concerned-looking, middle-aged woman in a white lab coat.

"I think there were a lot of different reasons," Mary said, lowering her eyes. "One of them, obviously, was that it felt so good. The first time, I mean. You never get the same buzz you do after the first time." She laughed miserably. "Pretty soon you stop getting any buzz at all. You just need it to feel normal. . . ."

She swallowed, shaking her head at the sordid images that were beginning to seep back into her mind: doing a clandestine blast in the parking lot of the DMV before her driving test, running off to the bathroom during final exams last spring, sneaking so much at her mother's birthday party that she got a nosebleed . . . and all the while justifying the behavior to herself by thinking: I'm just tired today. That's the only reason I'm doing it.

The problem was, she was tired every day.
And the exhaustion never let up.

"What was it like that first time?" Gaia asked.

Mary took a deep breath. "It was . . . wild. I went to this party with a guy I was dating—Brian Williams. I was a sophomore, and he was a senior. I guess I was kind of in awe of him." She smiled. "My parents hated him."

"Why?"

"He smoked. In front of my mom. He had long hair and lousy manners, and he dressed like a rock star. Seriously. The first time he came over here, he was wearing leather pants and this ripped black T-shirt. You could see his belly button though it. Which was pierced, by the way." She laughed again. "I thought he was glamorous."

"Go on," Gaia gently prodded.

"Anyway, he took me to this club downtown. I didn't know anyone there. It was all older people, friends of his from outside school. That band Fearless was playing."

"Really?" Gaia sat up straight. Her expression was strangely intense.

"Yeah. Why?"

"I just . . . I don't know." She shook her head. "That band just seems to haunt me."

Mary smirked. "I know what you mean. I'm strangely haunted by men named Chaz. Anyway, I barely heard them. Brian bumped into this friend of his." Her jaw tightened. "Guess who?"

203

"Skizz," Gaia whispered.

"The one and only." Mary closed her eyes and shuddered, feeling very much like she had been magically transported back to that stuffy, dimly lit basement. She could practically smell the smoke and hear the pounding beat of drums; she could see the creamy look of anticipation on Skizz's face.

"Anyway, he took us into one of the back rooms while the band was playing and got out a little envelope and a little spoon. He offered it to Brian first, then me. I was scared—but curious and excited, too. And I wanted to impress Brian, obviously. Plus it didn't seem like that big a deal. As far as I could tell, it didn't even affect Brian at all. He didn't freak out or anything. . . ."

Gaia leaned back against the pillows. "But it was a big deal." It was more of a question than a statement.

Mary opened her eyes again. "It was like I was suddenly transformed into this different person. I felt so cool. Really sexy, too—which was something I'd never felt before. And I thought I was in tune with everything that was happening around me. We went back out and danced, and I met a hundred different people. I wasn't shy or awkward at all." She cringed. "I probably made an ass of myself, but I had no clue."

Gaia nodded, but she didn't say anything.

Mary shook her head. It seemed so hard to believe that all the pain and lies and misery of the past year started right *there*—right at that exact moment. It was so random, in a way. What if she'd gotten sick that night and had never gone to the club? What if Skizz hadn't been there? What if she'd refused to go off with him? What if, what if . . . there were a thousand variations of the same question. Even when she was at the height of her addiction, she used to drive herself crazy asking herself what if.

"Needless to say, once that amazing feeling wore off, I went back for more," Mary continued. "All night long. I barely slept. I spent most of the next day crying. I didn't even know why I felt like such shit. But I had a feeling what could make me feel better." She sighed and glanced at Gaia. "I called Brian, and we hooked up with Skizz the very next night."

"And pretty soon Brian fell out of the picture," Gaia murmured. "Right?"

Mary nodded sadly. It was amazing how Gaia could see so much without having to be told. "I don't even know what happened to him. He just disappeared. You know what the crazy thing is? My parents were really psyched that he was gone. They thought I'd snapped out of a terrible, rebellious phase. They had no idea of the truth."

"But they do now," Gaia stated. "That's all that matters."

"Yeah, but . . ." Mary shook her head. She wished she could repeat Gaia's words with the same conviction. But she knew she couldn't. "The problem is, the demons don't go away that easily. They're always right there, right around the corner." Her voice fell to a whisper. "When things get bad, I still think about it—"

"Anytime that happens, call me," Gaia interrupted firmly. "I mean it. I don't care what time it is or where you are or anything. Just call me. I'll come." Her tone softened a little. "I'll come and kick those demons' asses."

Mary tried to return the smile. Her eyes began to smart. A tight knot grew in her throat. What had she done to deserve a friend like Gaia? How could she ever pay her back?

Actually . . . there might be a way.

Yes. She could do for Gaia what Gaia had done for her. She could help Gaia confront her *own* demons. Gaia couldn't go on keeping her entire past a secret. It wasn't healthy. Mary had known all along that something was eating at her friend, slowly destroying her. Everything pointed to it. Her eagerness to fight, her cocky attitude, her reluctance to get close to other people . . . they were all symptoms of something tragic, lurking just under the surface. And no matter how much fun she and Gaia had together, Gaia never lost that aura of wistful sadness—as if she were somehow certain that bad times were never far away.

So it was time for Gaia to tell the truth. And Mary would have to help her.

But she would have to be crafty. Crafty like Gaia. A simple, straightforward question wouldn't work. Gaia would never answer it. Plus they were still playing truth or dare. Mary would have to trick Gaia in the context of the game. Right. She'd have to trick Gaia in the same way Gaia had tricked *her* that night they'd snuck into Sam Moon's dorm. . . .

"So I guess it's your turn now, right?" Mary asked.

Gaia nodded.

"And you're obviously not gonna pick truth, right?"

Gaia nodded again, smiling.

"Then I *dare* you to tell me the truth," Mary said. She looked Gaia straight in the eye. "I dare you to tell me why you don't live with your family anymore."

FOR A MOMENT GAIA WAS FROZEN.

Fail-safe Point

Mary was smart. Gaia had known that from the day she'd met her. But she hadn't expected Mary to be so cunning. She hadn't expected Mary to beat her—fair and square, as the cliché went. There was nothing Gaia could do. She couldn't argue her way out of it; she couldn't fight her way out of it. She had to answer the question.

It was too bad Mary didn't know how to play chess. She'd be a hell of a chess player.

This marked one of those few times in Gaia's life that she was very happy to be the freak that she was. Because right now, fearlessness was a good thing. She wasn't afraid of talking about her family history. She wasn't afraid of digging up the past. Objectively, however, she knew it would cause emotional pain that she wasn't equipped to deal with. In a very real sense, it was like staring down the barrel of a loaded gun. She didn't have to feel fear to know that the gun would hurt her.

But for the first time she also knew that she didn't have to face the pain alone.

Until now she'd never been able to share the story of her family's demise because there had been nobody with whom to share it. It was that simple. She'd never had close friends. The string of foster families she'd lived with after her mother's death didn't give a rat's ass about anything except the support check from family services.

She had someone now, though. Somebody who would listen. Somebody who wouldn't judge her. Somebody who had also endured unspeakable suffering and shame—and had emerged stronger on the other side. Gaia owed it to herself to try. And to Mary.

"I . . . uh, it happened five years ago," she whispered.

Mary nodded.

The world seemed to melt away. The entire universe shrank to this room, this moment. Gaia stared into space, seeing nothing. Her mind was dominated by a vision of driving snow. . . .

"We used to spend time at this house in the mountains. We kind of lived there on and off," Gaia continued. "Just the three of us—me, my mom, and my dad. My dad worked—" Gaia broke off, clearing her throat. She wondered how much she should reveal about her father's business. Probably as little as possible, for the sake of Mary's safety. Not that Gaia had any concerns that this conversation would ever leave this room. She trusted Mary absolutely. Still, it was always best to be as cautious as possible. "My dad worked for a federal agency."

"Doing stuff he wasn't allowed to talk about, right?" Mary asked.

Gaia sighed. "Right." Mary understood perfectly. "So, anyway, the three of us lived in this cute little old house, way out in the boondocks. My mom always loved the country." Gaia swallowed. Her voice grew strained. "She . . . ah, she was from Russia originally. She grew up on a farm. Way up in the north. She loved the winters. . . . It was her favorite time of year." She shook her head, trying to wipe the image of her mother's face from her mind. "Anyway, my mom and dad never talked about my dad's work, although now I know that my mom must have been involved somehow. Or at least she *knew* everything. I mean, if she didn't know . . . she probably would have wondered why my father spent so much time teaching me all these exotic martial arts and forcing me to learn calculus."

Mary laughed softly. "That makes sense."

"Yeah." Gaia blinked several times. Again she saw that blanket of driving snow against a starless night sky. She felt like she was floating in a giant tub—and the drain had just been unplugged. She was swirling closer and closer to a dank, black hole. "So . . . there we all were, living up in this house . . . and—and it was winter, and . . ."

"It's okay," Mary murmured. "It's okay."

Gaia felt the wetness on her cheeks even before she realized she was crying. But she couldn't stop now. She was going to tell the whole story. Even if it killed her. She'd passed the fail-safe point. There was no turning back.

"It was night," she choked out. "There was a blizzard. We'd just finished dinner. My dad was setting up the chess table by the living-room window. We always played . . ." She sniffed. "We always played chess after dinner. My mom was in the kitchen, cleaning up. I was sitting across from my dad. Just looking out the window. I didn't see anything. Just snow. I didn't hear anything. Not a sound. I didn't . . ."

"It's okay," Mary repeated.

Gaia squeezed her eyes shut. No. It wasn't okay. It was anything *but* okay. The words seemed to come from somewhere else, as if Gaia were listening to a recording of herself speak. "There was a noise in the kitchen. A little twang, like the sound of a string being plucked. It was nothing. I didn't even think about it. Just a little twang. But my dad got this look in his eye. . . ." The pitch of Gaia's voice rose; the words came faster and faster. "He dove across the table and tackled me. All the chess pieces went flying. I screamed. I heard shooting. My dad was shooting at somebody. It was so loud. I tried to get up, but my dad held me down. I know it sounds stupid, but I thought I could help. I didn't know who was trying to hurt us or why, but I knew I had to save my mom and dad. Then the bullets stopped. My father got up. And—and . . ."

The next thing Gaia knew, she had collapsed into Mary's arms. She was sobbing uncontrollably. Her body shuddered. Her breath came in great heaving gasps. Mary said nothing. She simply held Gaia against her. Her grasp was very tight.

"I heard the sound of somebody running," Gaia wept. "But the thing I remember most was looking up—just for a second. Looking up, and seeing my dad in the doorway. And he looked at me. He was holding a gun. But his face . . . his face; there was nothing there. It was like a mask. Totally blank. His eyes were dead. . . ." She couldn't go on.

"What about your mom?" Mary whispered. "What happened to her?"

Gaia sniffed again, burying her face against Mary's shoulder. "I knew she'd been in the kitchen when the whole thing started. So I stood up and walked in that direction. I didn't see her at first. I thought maybe she was hiding, but . . . then I noticed the blood. It was all over the floor, leaving a trail that went behind the counter. When I turned the corner . . . she was just lying there. I sat next to her. I just put my head against her cheek and cried. My dad came in a little later, and—I don't know; we just waited. I don't really remember much else. An ambulance came and took us to the hospital. I rode up front. But it was too late. My dad and I just sat there in the waiting room all night, waiting for nothing. . . ."

Mary squeezed her tightly. "At least he was there for you."

Gaia struggled to take a breath. She shook her head. "He *was* there for me. But then he wasn't. When the doctors came out and told us that my mom had died, he didn't say anything. He just sat there, with those same dead eyes. Then he hugged me. It was a weird hug, though. It was like he was pulling me toward him and pushing me away at the same time. Neither of us spoke. And then . . . that was it. He got up and walked away. Of course, I thought he'd be back. I waited and waited. But I never saw him again. And I never found out what happened or why he left. After that, I went into foster care—"

"I'm so sorry," Mary whispered. "I'm so sorry."

Don't be, Gaia thought. Her body slowly started to relax. It was over. The night was over. The tears still came, and the pain still remained—but now there was something else, too. Relief. She never knew how right it would feel to express what had happened, to relive it. For the first time ever, she felt she could get over it. Of course, she knew she would never put it behind her completely—but she felt like she had somehow been set free.

"Are you okay?" Mary asked.

Gaia nodded. She leaned back and tried to smile once she managed to compose herself. "What do you say we stop playing truth or dare?"

Mary laughed softly. "I think that's a good idea." She glanced at the clock on her night table. It was almost 2 A.M. "You want to try to get some sleep?"

Gaia shook her head. "Nah. How about I teach you how to play chess instead?"

THE LISTENING DEVICE WAS GOOD FOR A

Neutralization

range of up to forty miles. Mary Moss's bedroom was no more than one-tenth that distance from the loft, so Loki had excellent reception.

He switched off the receiver and leaned back in his desk chair.

Well. That had been quite an enlightening little exchange. Quite an outpouring of emotion. Two girls, united by loneliness. Two misfits. Two outcasts. He shook his head. The bug had certainly proved its worth. It had been easy enough to plant; it was no bigger than a fingernail and practically transparent. And those so-called high-security buildings on Park Avenue were nothing of the sort. They could be easily penetrated in a variety of ways. Loki hadn't even needed a key. Earlier in the day he'd slipped undetected through the service entrance in the back. A third-rate burglar could have planted this bug.

He glanced up at the window and out at the Manhattan night. The city was alive this evening—crawling with people.

Of course. It was the holiday season.

Holidays meant nothing to Loki. As he saw it, they were arbitrary excuses for human beings to associate with one another. He was glad to be alone. He had always prized his solitude, but on nights like this—nights when he was forced to make an important decision—solitude was imperative.

He knew what would happen if Ella were here. She'd be clamoring for Gaia's head.

She'd insist that Gaia's breakdown tonight was evidence of deep-seated psychological instability and that Gaia would be of no use to them.

And she would be right . . . to a certain extent.

At the moment, in her current state, Gaia truly *was* of no use to them. She was of no use to anyone.

But Ella's insight only went so far. True, Gaia was unstable—but that was only because her environment was unstable. Every aspect of her life needed to be controlled. Rigidly. `Certain volatile factors needed to be eliminated.` Loki couldn't risk another outburst like that. Gaia was slipping further out of control. Too many secrets were at stake. Too many revelations were pending. So. There was no other possible course of action. He'd postponed the inevitable long enough.

Mary Moss had to be neutralized.

Immediately.

It's a shame, actually.

I know I am not what you wanted me to be. You would consider me heartless. And for that, I am a little bit sorry. But unfortunately, it was inevitable that I would become who I am.

Almost inevitable.

Once there was a chance that I could have been more. That chance was you, my love.

Katia.

Katia.

Even now my lips tremble as I speak your name. *Katia*. I would have sacrificed it all for you.

But that is not quite how things turned out. Instead you were stolen from me. And you went willingly, though I don't blame *you*. We both know who is really to blame.

That night. The last night I could still feel my heart beating in my chest. If only I had seen you there a moment earlier than I did. If only I could take back that one bullet that was meant

for someone else. If only you had
let me destroy Tom Moore instead
of trading your own life for his.

How I wanted to hold you as
you lay in that pool of blood. I
wanted to kiss those lips and
pull your soul into my own. And
how I've spent hundreds of
nights, playing it over and over
again in my head, thinking what I
should have done differently.

But as I have learned, there
is no time for regret. And there
is no time to chide you for loving my brother instead of me.
There is only time for revenge.

And believe me, Katia, revenge
is what I do best.

Everyone longs for something.
And everyone gives in to temptation sometimes.

Mary.

Heather.

Sam.

Now it's my turn.

Some secrets are too dangerous to know . . .

ROSWELL
HIGH

In the tiny town of Roswell, New Mexico, teenagers Liz Parker and Max Evans forged an otherworldly connection after Max recklessly threw aside his pact of secrecy and healed a life-threatening wound of Liz's with the touch of his hand. It turns out that Max, his sister Isabel, and their friend Michael are surviving descendants from beings on board an alien spacecraft which crash-landed in Roswell in 1947.

Max loves Liz. He couldn't let her die. But this is a dangerous secret he swore never to divulge - and now it's out. The trio must learn to trust Liz and her best friend Maria in order to stay one step ahead of the sheriff and the FBI who will stop at nothing in hunting out an alien...